SKUD

DENNIS FOON

SKUD

A GROUNDWOOD BOOK

DOUGLAS & McINTYRE

TORONTO   VANCOUVER   BERKELEY

Groundwood Books / Douglas & McIntyre
720 Bathurst Street, Suite 500, Toronto, Ontario
Distributed in the USA by Publishers Group West
1700 Fourth Street, Berkeley, CA 94710

We acknowledge for their financial support of our
publishing program the Canada Council for the Arts, the
Government of Canada through the Book Publishing Industry
Development Program (BPIDP), the Ontario Arts Council and the
Government of Ontario through the Ontario Media Development
Corporation's Ontario Book Initiative.

ONTARIO ARTS COUNCIL
CONSEIL DES ARTS DE L'ONTARIO

National Library of Canada Cataloguing in Publication
Foon, Dennis
Skud / by Dennis Foon
ISBN 0-88899-536-9 (bound).–ISBN 0-88888-549-0 (pbk.)
I. Title.
PS8561.O62S59 2003   jC813'.54   C2002-905169-X
PZ7
Library of Congress Control Number: 2002114433

Cover illustration by Joe Morse
Design by Michael Solomon

Printed and bound in Canada

For my daughters

TOMMY I spotted them in that acting class doing the talk talk. Sheila's smiling and laughing and the Scoob's laughing and smiling and then she gives him this little poke in the gut with her finger. He squeals like a pink pig and they put their arms around each other. Like wrapped. And their lips. Touch.

This is what I see. This is what my eyes burn into my brain forever.

I can't stand watching anymore. I slide down the hallway wall and wait. There's dust and crumbs and hairs blowing around me but I'm not caring. The hall is empty, there's no one to catch me broken like this. I hear their teacher saying words and clapping and more laughing and my head is pounding to explode. The bell rings and the pounding gets worse. Every throb in my head flashes white behind my eyes.

And here she comes.

I stroke my hand down her long blonde hair. She

7

SKUD

turns and looks at me, her green eyes cold. "Hey, Tommy."

Just hearing the sound come out of her lips slows the throbbing. I move her away from the crowd and smile at her. I want to be nice, say something like, you look great or I missed you, but all that comes out of my mouth is, "What were you doing with him?"

She stares at me like I'm whack and just shakes her head. "What do you care?"

"I care. You're my girl."

"No, Tommy. I'm nobody's girl."

I am blown down. My brain splatters into a thousand frags. "Are you breaking up with me?"

"No, Tommy, you broke up with me. De facto. You're gorgeous, Tommy, school hero, but I don't need a trophy. I want talk, communication."

"I talk to you all the time."

"But you never say anything. I don't know anything about you. I don't know who you are."

"Of course you do. I'm me. Everybody knows me."

"No, they don't. I don't think anybody does. I'm not even sure you do."

"But I love you."

"What does that mean?"

"Everything we do together. Everything we are. The swings at the park, bonfires at the beach, climbing the Grouse Grind…" I stop. My words are like .22 bullets against reinforced steel. She's impervious. I can't make a mark on her. My head starts to pound again.

The words crawl out of me. "It's the Scoob, isn't it?"

"Andy and me are just friends."

"I saw you and him. In there. What you were doing."

She peers at me with a strange look on her face, like I'm dim.

"That's called acting, Tommy. Acting." And she walks away, leaving me in the cold, cold hallway, people all chuckles and jokes jostling to their next class.

Somebody shouts my name. "Hey, Tommy Man!" The chill runs through me. Did they see? Did they hear her words? Are they laughing?

"Congratulations," the somebody says, thumping me on the back. "You made the Honor Roll again!"

"When did that get announced?" I ask.

"Mr. Gee leaked it. He was bragging about you in class again and let it slip."

I shake my head.

"Hey, don't let it get up your ass, man, you did good."

"You're the best, bud!" somebody else says, and they're all smiling and slapping me and reminding me I'm number one.

I grin and wink and wave and put on that face that everybody likes. No one knows my head is pounding like a dying V-8, light blasting behind my eyes.

She dumped. Me.

SKUD

There's a kind of pain I love. A pain that feels so wondrous it makes me want to scream. I can't sit, I can't stand, I can't lie down because the pain is surging through me. I'm on the machine, doing super high-rep training, fifty straight tricep extensions. Everything in me is burning, screaming, crying, but I dig down, flushing my triceps, totally annihilating them.

Then I collapse. Numb. I feel nothing, the greatest feeling in the world. My sweat's a hot pool underneath me on the black vinyl bench. I hear the drip, drip, drip of it on the floor. I open my eyes a little and see myself in the wall-to-wall mirrors that surround the gym.

I look incredible. I look like someone in lactic-acid buildup pain, someone who's doing everything right. My skin tone is superb, not a pimple in sight, because I know how to administer the pills.

Brainless imbeciles gobble the steroids, they rush to dump the body fat, swell the chest, bulk the biceps. Sure, they score the muscle, along with zits and tits. No lie, I've seen body builders who look like Mr. Universe – with hooters. I don't know how they can stand looking at themselves in the mirror. That is not a problem I will ever have. I can look at myself all day and not throw up because I am delighted with what I see. I'm on the road to perfection.

My bud Tommy walks in as I'm starting my bench presses. He's standing straight-backed and strong-jawed, every molecule of his skin the officer-to-be. But old soldier boy can't fool me. His eyes are red and puffed out like an aquarium fish. In my humble opinion, he's been crying. Of course, admit this he would never do. Tommy is the rock, he who never is shaken, perfect manners, perfect gentleman. This is good and bad. When Tommy's upset, he's dangerous, unpredictable, a walking incendiary. A side I, his closest friend, have only seen once before – something to do with his hag of a mother.

"You're upset," I say, wondering if this family thing has come back to haunt him.

"No, I'm fine," replies he.

"Your eyes look bee-stung, mosquito-bit. You are in pain."

"No, I am not."

I lift my neck and stare at him. "We are like brothers, joined at the hip. Spew forth."

He stands there at attention, his body tight. I sit up and lock on him, matching his silence with mine. Finally he spills.

"Brad, man, she and me, it's over."

"Over? You were the perfect couple. Mr. and Mrs. Beautiful and Amazing. I thought you two had a love that was never-ending."

"We did. And now we don't."

Am I surprised? No, because this pure love notion is highly overrated and hazardous. People are always diving into it and they end up crashing on the rocks below. My colleague, beneath that taut

SKUD

military exterior, is a passionate soul. I hate to see him suffer.

So I ask, "Why did you dump her?"

Tommy looks at me, both eyes glistening. "I didn't."

"So this was a mutual?"

His eyes burn holes in his feet.

"Tell me."

After a year, he speaks.

"I was dumped," he says.

"Sheila dumped you?"

"Truth," saith he. Then he peers at me. "Why the face?"

"What face?" I ask, pushing two hundred pounds over my head.

"You're smiling," he notes, and he's right, I am.

"The grin comes from the joke," I admit. "You're joking, I'm smiling,"

He shakes his head. "It's no joke."

Now I'm laughing. I practically drop the bar on my neck I'm laughing so hard. "You want me to believe this? Dumped? You? The prince of the school? Fighter pilot to be?"

He sits down beside me on the bench. "Truth, truth, truth!" he mutters.

This is nonsense of the tenth degree. This I cannot compute. "Tell, me, Tombo, explain why you clung to that skrunky piece till she gave you the heave."

Tommy turns radioactive, ready to nuke. "What did you call her?"

I quickly rephrase. "Sorry, don't get me wrong, I didn't mean it like that. I know you cared."

"I loved her, man."

"I still wonder why you didn't see it coming."

He shakes his head. "Love blinded me. She was mine."

I'm bewildered. Tom-Tom's a formidable ally, a boy-man with a future, with wings. But he is not whole. This is because he's got no one to show him life. Thus I take him under my wing. Who else is there to give him help, advice and comfort?

"I keep telling you, Tommy. Love 'em all. That is fine, that is good. But if you relax on the defense, your team gets shredded. I love them, pal, but none of them, nobody, ever gives me the heave."

"Well, I've been heaved, Brad. Totally." And Tommy sits down next to the bench, the little scar on his cheek looking dead white on his pallid skin. I put my arm around him and give his wiry shoulder a pat.

"Don't worry about it, Tom. Just remember next time. Always leave them begging for more. Then get on the next bus. Like I always say, pop 'em and chop 'em."

These are golden words of advice, not ones I share with every passerby. But, Tommy, he's my bud. And you have an obligation in this world to help your buds whenever possible, circumstances permitting.

"Don't dog out on me, Tomster. It's bad, sure, you got the chop. But at least you gave her the pop, right?"

13

SKUD

Tommy gapes at me. The scar on his face is starting to shine.

An unsettling thought floats into my mind. "You did pop her, didn't you?"

Tom-Tom's not quick to reply. "It's not gentlemanly to answer questions like that."

His face goes dark. There's more to this thing than meets the eye. I detect some humiliating substance on my tormented friend. He can't look at me when he says it.

"I didn't just get chopped."

Oh, man. I'm getting an uncomfortable feeling. You'd think I taught him something after all these years. "More than chopped? How does one get more than chopped?"

Tommy sadly nods. "I was MG'd."

I'm stunned. The blood is curdling in my veins. "MG'd?"

"I was MG'd major."

I can't believe it. His face has been rubbed in it and scraped off. Somebody stole his One and Only. Not ace. Not funny. Not good.

"Who made you the goat?" I ask, and I'm starting to feel a little heated. But Tommy's not forthcoming. He doesn't want to tell. I press the case and finally he spits it out.

"Andy."

Andy! Big Andy the fullback! Six foot five, three hundred bad-tempered pounds. Big Andy crushes bone for the fun of it. Even with Tommy's military training, he'd be no match for that behemoth. His MG is suddenly transformed from deadly insult to simple bad luck.

"Big Andy? You're lucky to have escaped unscathed, pal. What Big Andy wants, he takes, and those of the living step aside. This is not tragedy, my prince. This is horseshoes up your butt."

But Tommy's pride is not soothed by my giving his ego a clean bill of health, which is puzzling. There is no shame in this. He had no alternative but to step away and let Big Andy take his girl.

"It wasn't Big Andy," he sighs.

I'm puzzled.

"It was the other Andy," he says.

I have to contemplate this statement. There is another Andy in our grade, but this is barely an Andy with a name.

"The other Andy? You're saying she ditched you for the other Andy?" Then it hits me like a stinking, rotting fish. "You mean Andy the Scoob? The one who wears tights in the auditorium?"

Tommy, completely humiliated, nods. "That's the perpetrator."

I am aghast, stunned, sickened. This tale is getting more pitiful by the second.

"That Andy doesn't even have pistons, Tom. He's not like onside, you know what I mean? Anyway, I thought Andy was a tomato."

"So did I. But apparently Sheila's not in agreement."

Suddenly the situation is different. Suddenly bloody retribution is called for. The honor of my man is at stake.

"What are you gonna do about it?" I inquire. "What's gonna happen to Andy the actor?" I look deep in his eyes. Down in the bottom of those pits, I see a little flame start to catch fire, the knives opening up inside him.

"What action is called for?" he asks, and my heart rises an inch.

"The guy's a twig, Tom. Snap him in two."

He shakes his head. "You know I can't do that."

"Like spare me, right? It's a sleepwalk. There's naught to do here but a quick stomp. The big question for this party is what shoes to wear."

"It's a public event. I can't be seen doing such things."

"Under the circumstances, you can't not be seen doing this thing."

"It's strictly against the code."

"You're not gonna get reprimanded for an honorable action."

"But it's an unfair contest."

"Oh, come, come, compadre. Is it fair for this freak to smear your face in front of the world?"

"I'm supposed to let things like this go."

"What do you think the military's about?"

"Protecting freedom."

I point at him. "Exactly! And when freedom is endangered, the armed services step up. Well, your freedom and honor and dignity have been threatened, my friend. The enemy just attacked your borders."

I can see we are making progress. He was already warm to the idea. He just needs some help with the details.

"You have to draw the line in the sand. Make it very clear to the world that no more trespasses will be tolerated. If you do not, there will be a feeding frenzy. The enemy will pick your bones."

Tommy shakes his head, relenting. "It has to be done very low profile."

"Slate it for a half hour after the bell so nobody comes."

"That might work," he nods. "So are you my backup?"

"Backup for what?"

"Just in case, you know. In case he has some."

Now I'm laughing. "What kind of backup does a tomato get? A couple of cantaloupes and a cucumber? Maybe he'll bring the other actors with him. What were they doing, the Wizard of Oz? Be afraid, friend, the Scoob'll have Munchkins for backup."

Tombo is laughing too. "Okay, okay, it's my training, all right? You gotta prepare for every contingency."

I give him a pat. "I'll be there. Not because you need me or anything for this tomato squash thing, but to keep an eye on things. Make sure no powers that be are there to witness. This way you can get

SKUD

your face back but not lose your stripes for the indiscretion. I'll be an observer, you know. All peace and love."

Tommy gazes at me. "And if anything goes wrong?"

I grin. "Then we bomb the shit out of him."

 The roof of the school is my favorite place. From up here, everything down there looks like little insects. The football field's swarming with army ants tackling each other. The grass on the side's infested with earwigs chasing the ladybugs, and a more futile mating ritual I have never seen. The gravel pit is filled with paper termites burrowing through their books. And due south is the Cage, where a fence full of moths have been drawn to a bright light. A pair of fireflies are burning up an innocent dung beetle. Not a pretty sight.

Up here's a bug-free zone, except for me. I am doing my diction exercises. This means I'm repeating a phrase over and over. Everybody would think I'm weird if they caught me in the act. But it is much harder than it looks.

Go on. You try saying it.

Pretty princess primped and pricked the prone potatoes. Prone potatoes pretty to primp she pricked and picked.

You think it's easy? Go on, try it. Say it out loud. Start slow, then faster and faster. Harder than it looks, isn't it?

My acting coach gave it to me. Exercises your mouth. He says your head is one big resonator, like a stereo speaker. Use it! Use every square inch of your head! I thought he was full of it until I found out he co-starred in two movies with Mel Gibson. He is an actual close personal friend of Steven Spielberg. He got us screen tests and had them sent down to Steve to be critiqued. Spielberg – well, his executive assistant said I have talent.

My long-term plan is this. Audition, audition, audition. Get on a TV show, like Johnny Depp did in the beginning. Do it for a few years, get the exposure, put money in the bank, then flip into features. I'll co-star a lot, build up the rep, then start producing for myself. This is the key part of the plan. You produce it so you keep the profit. You keep the control. Schwarzenegger, Mel Gibson, Jackie Chan, they own the product. Nobody pays them one million and walks away with a hundred and fifty. Arnie, Jackie, they take half. Or more.

Nothing in life is secure. But ninety million dollars would really help a lot, don't you think?

"Hey, very scary, Scoob. No fear of heights."

The voice makes me lurch 'cause the roof is my oasis, my private studio. Once I was visited by the janitor but never before has a bug from below invaded my sanctuary.

SKUD

I turn to see local hero Tommy Mao looking at me. Tommy is the school's top military boy, on track to join the air force, which these days is quite the status number. He sometimes hangs outside acting class. I keep meaning to ask how he gets the boots so shiny, but we were never properly introduced.

"Welcome to my getaway. You're Tommy, right? I guess heights like this are chicken feed to a high flier."

I never noticed that Tommy has a weird little scar on his cheek. Makes him look slightly diabolical. I note it for future reference. I could use it if I ever play Richard III.

He gives me this intense look. "What do you do up here, Scoober?"

"My name's Andy," I say. Scoober is the nickname the insect community has been trying to pin on me. Maybe it's the acting thing. Do I like it? No. "I'm doing diction exercises," I reply.

His chin nods and keeps nodding like a bobble doll in a car's back window. It's a peculiar movement, worth remembering. He moves closer.

"You make me puke, pin head."

This is actually the first time I've had a conversation with Tommy, who is universally considered a reasonable, polite and level-headed fellow. But this is not what I am seeing. This guy is all glassy-eyed and making threatening Neanderthal noises, which is probably unfair to Neanderthals, who were apparently much more sociable than our school hero is at the moment.

"Is there a problem?" I smile and keep my palms open to give him the body language of calm.

"You are the problem," he snarls, looking like a predator. "You crossed the line."

"I'll give you some room then, okay?" I decide a hasty retreat is the best medicine. A plan with potential, except for the part about him blocking the door.

"Trespass." His hands shoot out, shoving me. I fly back and hit the wall. This is a dirty wall, and my shirt, once clean and yellow, is now covered in grime.

"Hey," I say, bewildered at his transformation from Dr. Jekyll to Mr. Hyde. "What's your problem?"

Tommy's face is turning red like a beet. The scar looks like a little white raft floating in the Red Sea. He looks like Moses before he hurled the Ten Commandments.

"You," he says. "Nobody MG's me."

Now I'm at sea. MG? Me MG him? The phrase implies I am bedding with someone he loves. Which is impossible, given the fact that I'm the only person I've ever slept with. Scoff. Laugh. Mock. Go ahead, fling your stones at me. I can take it. I can take anything. Obviously you know nothing about the power of Tantric yoga.

Vaguely hoping to maintain my dignity, I ask flyboy who he might be referring to. His scar nearly lifts off his head when he hisses the name. Sheila.

This big gulpy laugh explodes out of my throat. "Sheila?"

SKUD

His eyes go narrow, a cobra about to strike. "She was mine," he mutters.

Admission: I am thrown. Confession: I do sleep with Sheila. Every night. In my mind. Sad note: She doesn't know it. You see, she's the object of my Tantric yoga discipline. Even in my fantasies we've never consummated. That's where the discipline comes in. The objective is to bring yourself as close as possible to the zenith and stop yourself. By mastering this kind of control, not only do your sheets stay dry, you can gain unsurpassed personal power and charisma, both essential qualities for the successful actor.

For an unsettling moment I wonder if I'm in trouble because of my fantasies. Is Tommy psychic? Has he entered my astral plane and witnessed my yogic struggles?

Then it hits me. "Tommy. Sheila and me act together. That's it. Nothing more."

"Don't play me, actor man. I saw it all."

"This is nuts, Tommy. We were doing a scene."

He eyes me. Sizes me. Inhales some air. "You talk to her?"

I relax a little. "Sure, yeah, a bit."

"And what does she say about me?"

I'm on dangerous ground. Anything I say could provoke this maniac. Do I say nothing? Say a little? Tell all? I mean, Sheila talked to me once about him. Told me how perfect and god-like he is. Good-looking, smart, athletic and well mannered. But he doesn't talk to her about anything, she complained. She said he was like the sphinx.

I am not a sphinx, I wanted to tell her, but I knew no matter how unsphinx-like I may be, my match would never light her firecracker.

But the immediate threat is before me. For the sake of self-preservation, I opt to speak only what is public knowledge.

"She never said anything that isn't already on the street, Tommy. You two are finished."

He whispers so I can barely hear. "She was mine."

The volcano is ready to blow. My brain races to find a way to douse the fire. If he's looking for battle, I am not his man. Understand, my career depends on my face and teeth. Remember the actor who played Luke Skywalker? Mark Hamill's face was wrecked in a crash and his career tanked. I'm not wrecking my future. I've sworn never to fight unless it's been rehearsed by a certified fight choreographer, and I doubt that Tommy's here for rehearsal.

He moves closer.

"She said you had no interest in her," I tell him. "It was over."

I immediately wish I could vacuum the words as they spill from my lips. His eyelids go drowsy, hang there like the practice gliders he flies in the sky.

Then he says, "You want interest? Here."

I don't see it coming. One fist to the gut and I'm down. At least he didn't hit my face.

23

SKUD

"After school," he says, "in the Cage." And he's gone.

As much as I loathe it, I have no choice. The rule is you take the challenge or get swarmed when you're least prepared. My best hope to protect the parts dearest to me is going *mano a mano*.

I lie there forever trying to get a breath. Sheila keeps popping into my mind. Stroking my back, massaging my head, crying at my grave. He slugged me thinking she and I are one. We're not, but now, sitting here all bent up, stomach heaving, I feel closer to her than ever.

Then I feel a tremor and a dark cloud passes over me.

It's a shadow. A gigantic shadow.

Is it the janitor, come to ban me from the roof? No, worse. The principal, here to expel me from this crumbling school? No, much, much worse.

Shane. One of the leaders of the TMR gang. Car thief, arsonist, drug dealer, killer. I myself just three months ago saw him in action. I was safely ensconced up here in my perch after hours and looked down. Shane is arguing with some guys in a car. In a blink, he pounds the driver's face into bloody pulp, then somehow sets the car on fire. Two guys, in flames, run screaming out of the vehicle but Shane is gone, nowhere to be seen.

He is an animal.

So, you might ask, why is such a multi-talent psychopath still attending school? In a word, alibi.

It's a perfect set-up, really. Everyone's terrified of him, even the teachers. He cuts class, goes out to wreak havoc and destruction on the innocent. After he's robbed, burned, mugged or beaten whoever stepped in his path, he returns to class to do his math assignment. If the police come asking, nobody's going to tell on him. Not a student, not a teacher. Legend has it that little Miss Post, the sweet and friendly and very old English teacher, ratted on him last year. They say he opened the door for her, smiled, then threw her down the third-floor stairs. She's had complications from her back surgery and both hips replaced. But her broken arm's healed up really well, I hear.

Now the victim is not Miss Post or the guys in the burning car. It is me.

He studies me with this cold look in his eyes, detached like a surgeon, sizing me up for the kill. My life may soon be over, but I can't help but be fascinated. It's the closest I've ever been to a real-life villain.

Involuntarily, I study his moves. He's incredible.

"Do you want this space?" I ask. "This entire roof is totally yours. I'm just leaving."

I pull myself up and head for the door. But he takes a step toward me, and I freeze. I don't run, don't want to turn. If I'm facing him he can't shoot me in the back.

I stare at his feet (black, scuffed, metal-tipped boots) and say as humbly as I can, "No offence intended. May I give you a small gift?"

SKUD

I go for my wallet but stop because he moves closer. I can feel his eyes on me, staring at my face. So close I smell the expensive cologne. I think his nose may have been broken once. Three earrings on the right ear, one big gold ring on the left. Scars on his hands.

From knife fights? Broken glass? Punching skulls?

He comes even nearer, so close I can smell spearmint on his breath, and now I'm squeezing myself trying not to leak down my leg. Why of all days am I being thrown to the wolves today? From frying pan to fire and now I'm fated to burn. What's my crime? What's he after? With his type a look is enough, or being in the wrong place, or he just doesn't like your face – my only thing of value.

"I only have ten bucks," I squeak.

He shakes his huge, shaven head.

"Thought you were somebody else," he shrugs. And he goes.

I sit there and watch the baddest of all bad make his exit. And I feel a kind of wonder fall over me.

He thought I was somebody. Me. Somebody.

To say the least, an interesting day. To say the most, I'm still alive. Until the Cage.

BRAD

My cohort Tommy has his heart set on the air force. He's obsessed with flying up there in the water vapor. Me, I like my water solid. Ice. I'm being scouted as we speak for Junior A. I'll score the pros because whatever it takes, I'm willing to do. Gouge your eyes, kick, spear, smash noses into jelly. That's the game. Get the advantage, get the big contract. When my moment comes, I will not sign for less than six figures. That means after five years of pro, I'm set for life. Because I know the secrets to success. Key: Never apologize. Never a hint of weakness. You have to be totally sure about what you're doing. Listen to no one. Take no prisoners. This is a lesson I endeavor to teach the Tomster.

Hockey understands me. And I understand hockey. My dad's had me on ice since I was four. I slide, I fly, I crash, I smash. This is what he taught me. This is what I do.

Dad of mine never misses a game. Always sits in the same place, first row center ice. He carries rocks in his pockets to throw at referees who make bad calls. Dear old Dad was a pitcher. He has no knees, so he knows how to use his wrists. Never once have they seen the rock coming. If they trained like me, they'd see it.

We used to practice behind the garage. Me in shorts and T-shirt, with only my stick for protection. He has a bucket of stones. He throws, I have to deflect them. I smack the rock or the rock smacks

SKUD

me. He throws hard. If I whimper, he throws harder.

Once I took my stick and I knocked down a bee's hive. Just to see if I could. Whether I could take it or not. I got thirty-two stings. It was nothing compared to those stones. My dad trained me well.

I sit on the bench putting on gear, my shining armor. Elbow pads, the legacy of Gordie Howe, the invisible lance to the enemy's ribs. Hip pads for the joust, a flick, and to the boards the opponent flies. Knee pads, so if I topple, instead of hurting me, whoever I land on gets hurt. Shin pads to deflect the bulleting puck and the cup to save the jewels. My blades are razor-sharp swords, my helmet turns my head into a battering ram.

While I solemnly don my suit of mail, Coach comes to me and gives me a slap on shoulder. Coach was once a pro. Three years with Detroit. Now he is fat. But I respect him. He gives me lots of ice time, likes me best when I pillage and destroy.

"Ready for practice?" Coach says.

"Always," I shrug.

"Work on your speed."

"All the better to check with," I smile.

He sighs and sits down on the bench across from me and leans back against a locker. His nose looks redder than usual.

"You look tired," I say.

"Politics," he says. "Every job's got politics." He horks in his throat. Pulls out a big red handkerchief and gobs into it. Used to be he'd just spit in the drain but the powers that be frowned on this.

"They want more wins?" I ask.

He shakes his head.

"They want more everything. They're changing the game on me. You see my ass? There is the pain. They are that pain."

His butt is huge, so his pain, I calculate, is proportional. He sits, quiet like, then shakes his head and stands up. Looks at me, then gives me a shot on the shoulder.

"You're a good man, Brad," he says. "Keep up the good work."

I feel no comfort from those words. Bile is rising in my gut. A burning, a dread.

What the hell was that about? How is the game changing? Something's worrying him and now it's worrying me. Did I fail him somehow? Am I sitting on a crumbling throne? I watch him waddle off.

I shrug it off. We both know I'm irreplaceable. This team was feeble before I arrived and whipped it into shape. I'm his fist, his blade, his heart. I'm only feeling butterflies because my stomach always goes knotty before I hit the ice, that's all. Look at him. A tired, worried bag of flesh. What burden was he dumping on me? Wife problems, probably. He's fat, so she's MG'ing him. He should lose some weight, pump some iron. Must be tough going old and wide. I'd blow my brains out before I'd ever let that happen to me.

SKUD

TOMMY Here I am, library locked, until 15:30. Then I exit this quiet world and report to the Cage to fulfil my obligations.

This library is more home than home. This place is tranquillity. Here there are books on planes, on flight. Here people speak in whispers. Here the secret light flashing behind my eyes stops strobing. No one knows how much I like this cubicle, surrounded by encyclopedias, thick wall of pages around me.

Here, in my cubicle, I think about the Art of Survival. That's what the military's all about. Dodging shells. Weapons handling. Search and rescue. Freeing hostages with gunships.

Next year I move to the island to train as a fighter pilot. I'll be flying F-16s. See the world. At twice the speed of sound. Once you're strapped in, you're the jet, the jet is you. Not virtual reality. Reality reality. It's you. You plug into it. Become One. The oxygen, the communications. Computer at your fingertips. Only now, you're not this skin and bone, this weakness, this nothing. Now your skin is titanium. Your ears are enhanced radar. Your eyes are infrared thermal sights. You move stratospheric. You have smart bombs, glide bombs, Maverick missile-seeker heads. Boom. You hit the speed of sound once. Boom. You hit it twice. And you keep going. You're passing one thousand two hundred klicks an hour, one thousand three hundred, four hundred, five hundred. And nothing stops you, nothing touches you. You are untouchable.

"Tommy?"

I look up and see Mr. Gee, my physics and science teacher. The sour egg breath on him pulls me back and I grimace at the thick hairs sprouting from his nose and ear holes. But I would never let him know that.

"What's wrong, son? Your eyelids were fluttering."

I chuckle. "How embarrassing, sir. I must've dozed off." I am always the good-natured student.

"I had a dog that slept with his eyes open once. Eyelids fluttered just like that."

"What happened to him?"

"We had to put him down."

"I hope you're not thinking about that for me!"

Mr. Gee laughs, slaps me on the shoulder, his eyes narrowing on the paper that sits in front of me. "I see you're still trying to crack that projectile motion problem."

"Yes, it's a tough one, sir. But I'm working on it."

To fly, you need physics. This is my best class. I look at his face. His eyes go in different directions because one eye is blind. I don't know which eye to look at, so I focus on his chin.

"You'll get it, if anybody can. You've got a great attitude, Thomas. You remind me of me."

"I'm flattered to hear you say that, Mr. Gee."

"Congratulations for making the Honor Roll again, Thomas. Of course, it was no surprise."

SKUD

"Thank you, sir."

For a second I wish this half-blind man could see through me. But I know he can't. His one eye sees the same as everybody else. The good boy, the hero boy. Why doesn't he notice the way my head is splitting right now? He's a teacher, a scientist. If he could look inside my skull he'd see how twisted up my nerves are, his eyes would be singed by the flaring sparks of my brain. My brain is bad right now. It's on fire, practically burning him, but he doesn't feel it. No one does.

The throbbing in my cortex starts again. I'm late for the Cage.

 They call it the Cage but it's really just a backstop. Fastballs the catchers miss blast into the mesh. The ground around home plate is covered in gravel. I hate gravel. The pebbles always get in your shoes.

In a half hour, anyone still present will come to see the bloodbath. My bloodbath. The audience will be standing room only. Very Ancient Rome, pure Coliseum and gladiators. In this case, I'm the bait they're throwing to the lions. I'm not completely unprepared, though. I have Master Shum's Introduction to Martial Arts on cassette, and I'm plugged into the great man's actual voice.

The instruction manual, complete with cassette, was a present from my dad before he died. This and *The Joy of Sex*. We never discussed either subject when I was growing up. Then about two years ago, he got throat cancer and had about a month to live.

Everybody was a big mess about it. My mom still is. All she does is work and take Prozac. She's totally wrecked. For me the whole thing was a dream. I was numb, kind of like being stoned, floating in a daze. I just zombied through it all, like my eyes were crossed or something.

In the hospital, he's lying there looking all bald and emaciated, almost like he was an extra in *The Night of the Living Dead*. You don't want to get too close to those monsters, because if they bite you, you turn into one too. I can hear his lungs rattling and he's gasping for air, even with the oxygen mask. He lifts a white bony finger and motions me closer. I inch over to him and he motions to a bag on the table.

I reach inside, and there they are: Master Shum's book with cassette and *The Joy of Sex*. Like it was a little late, you know what I mean? Most guys learn these things at puberty. But not me. My dad was never around. Always on the road. Or reading newspapers. I saw more of him that last month in the hospital than I did my whole life.

And even then it wasn't like we had long conversations. After all, he didn't have a throat. But he'd write me little notes. My favorite one took him

SKUD

about ten minutes to write because he was so jammed from the morphine. It had three words on it. Ten minutes for three words: Be a Man. That's the whole thing – be a man. Only problem: he didn't tell me how you do that. I guess he figured everything you need to know on the subject is summed up in these two books.

Anyhow, he died a day after writing the three words. So I guess he thought they were pretty important.

"From open palm, fold fingers," says the voice of Master Shum. "Place thumb on top of index and middle fingers." I'm wondering what the hell he's talking about when his voice says, "See Illustration 5B."

I pick up the instruction manual that comes with the tape and find Illustration 5B. It's a picture of a fist. Sad fact: I have to take a course to learn how to make a fist.

"Keep wrist even with forearm," says the great one, and I take a guess as to what that means.

"Weight on right foot, lunge forward and punch. Again. Again."

I do as instructed, three more times – not an easy task when you have no clue if you're doing it right. I guess I should be pleased with my progress. I didn't fall once.

BRAD

Tom Boy's still in the library, his favorite haunt. We picked the time for the event strategically. Just long enough after dismissal to be sure the teachers have gone home but enough of a crowd to make sure Tom's message gets through.

I see Mr. Gee talking to him and I watch the teacher leave with an uppity nod at me. The maestro puts a pain up my butt. He with the hate for the pills. He with the contempt for those who will be strong. He with the statistics and test results. Gee never misses the chance to remind me that they tested steroids on rats and the poor rodents died horribly. Rats are not people, Mr. Gee. Rats cannot read the warnings, Mr. Gee, rats do not know their dose. Look at me. No zits, no tits. No pain, no gain. He's always the long term, the long term. All from a one-eyed chump who rides a bicycle to work. Pedal on, Mr. Gee. Talk to me when I get drafted NHL.

Finally the clock strikes and my brother-in-arms rises.

"Hey, Tom-Tom," says I. "What's gonna happen to the Scoob?"

He gives me a nervous look and has a quick scan around to see if anybody heard my quip.

"This isn't something we're broadcasting."

"You're right. I'm sorry but my mind keeps wandering, wondering about the plan of attack."

"I'm on it," is all Tommy says, and after that he

SKUD

stays mum as we walk around the school and head toward the Cage.

"You're tense, my man, you are overwrought."

"No, I'm not," he says, but he is, and we both know it.

"Listen, the weather is nice and crisp. And like I expected, by not starting the show right after the bell, we lost a big chunk of the potential audience. Which is what you were hoping for, right?"

"Right," he nods, the tension steaming off him.

Only six or seven snaps are there and a couple of skrunks who interest me not. Most important, no authority figures in sight. Scoob is already present, doing his own preparations, making some Jet Li punches at an invisible enemy. With every punch he loses his balance and stumbles. I laugh but Tommy goes cold at the sight. He is actually wondering if this Scoob routine might be reality and if he will have to exert himself to put the tomato away.

I use calming words to ease Tom's distress.

"Relax, Tombo. Just go make nice with the boy." And I step over to the Scoob, just to shake him a little off the top. "Hey, it's Mr. Kung Fu."

Andy the tomato does his best to remain calm.

"You're late," saith he. Suddenly he's a kung fu man and an alarm clock all wrapped in one.

"What kind of game is this, Scoob? Does this kung fu shit mean you want to play rough?"

"I didn't get the impression you were playing," the actor says, staring at Tommy with his eyes bulging out, trying to act the samurai warrior, but looking more like a bag lady.

"So what's with the black belt thing, Scoober?" I ask. "You got your diploma?"

"Yeah," he lies. "Fourth degree."

This makes me laugh but not Tommy. Tomster's face has gone red, he is so cranked with hate for this worm. I try to focus him a little.

"Hey, Tom. Here. Take my diploma."

I unbuckle my belt and slide it out of the loops.

"This belt is historical," I announce, loud enough for the fence-sitters to hear. "This belt was once owned by Jacko Tractor, the meanest biker in Vancouver. Jacko's the guy who threw that kid off the seawall over some dope thing. They tried putting him in prison again but not one of five hundred people who saw the deed would testify."

My belt is three inches wide. It is covered in sharp metal studs. I hand my favorite accessory to my pal.

"You know, Tommygun, I think this cantaloupe lacks backup. In fact, I believe he is one big lack."

This has the desired effect on Tommy. The crooked little grin I love so much cracks across his lips and he begins swinging the belt around, moving closer to Scoobsky, who is becoming very nervous. He takes three small backward steps.

A snap on the fence shouts, "Hit him!"

"Come on," saith Tommy to the wilting Scoob. "Let's have a black belt demonstration."

"Ditch the leather and I will," replies smart-

SKUD

mouth. But Tommy doesn't comply. Instead, he showily snaps the belt in the air, nowhere near Scoob, but the tomato still dives for cover.

"Get up," Tommy orders, like a boot camp sergeant. "Stand up!"

Andy the Scoob warily rises and as soon as his feet are on the ground, Tommy lashes the belt again in the air. Once more the Scoob hits the dirt, terrified. By now the peanut gallery is in stitches, laughing their asses off at this pathetic stooge.

"Do something!" Tommy tells him. "Come on." And Tommy nudges Scoob with his boot. Scoob goes lower. Tom dangles the belt around his ears, tickling his neck. Andy tries to worm away. The watchers on the fence are yelling insults at the Scoob, whose face is pinched, fighting tears, having proved himself to be a complete invertebrate.

But then something happens. Somehow Scoob manages to reach up, catch the belt in his hand and yank it away.

The Scoob has made a fatal error. He stole my belt.

"Hey, give it!" says Tommy, but Scoober just shakes his head.

"No," says he.

This is not good. This does not make my day. I take four slow, long steps toward the criminal.

"That's my personal wardrobe, Scoober," I pronounce.

Scoober, like some cornered hound, eyeballs me.

"For a truce," he says. I can't help but laugh.

"My belt for your life?"

"Correct."

I turn to Tombo. "He's good, he's really good. Scoobie Doober drives a hard bargain, Tom."

Tommy's face frowns. He grimaces at Scoob. "All you do is take what's not yours," he snarls.

I move closer to our victim. "I have had enough of this crust. I paid sixty bucks for this belt and he wants even trade. Oh, do I hate being jacked."

My arm lightnings out and my hand grips the Scoob by the neck. He makes a small gurgling sound. I push his face into the gravel. Very softly, I speak to him.

"Give me what's mine," I say, soft as velvet. Scoober, without hesitation, quickly gives me the belt.

But now I'm feeling playful. "Continue," I demand, letting him up. "Interest. You owe me."

He shudders. "Take what you want," he says, trying to be brave.

"I want everything," say I, with a friendly smile parting my lips like a shark's fin cutting water.

I nod to Tommy and he removes the jacket off Actor Boy.

"It's black, my favorite color," I state. "Persevere," I say to Tomster, nodding at the boots.

"I just got these," Scoobie squawks. Tommy waves his finger. Scoob removes the boots and hands them over.

SKUD

"More," I say. The Actor does not move, unsure of what is being asked for. I hit him in the eye and Scoob suddenly understands. He takes off his shirt and pants.

Our audience on the fence is hooting, shouting, laughing. This is the most applauded performance of the Andy's career. I should have charged admission for the show. And Scoob's costume is perfect now. Just underpants. He is shivering.

"We'll let you keep the gonch, Scoob," say I. "Unless you'd like us all to check for skid marks."

"No, thanks," Andy the naked actor replies.

"Gee, I'm starting to feel shopped out. What time is it, Scoob?"

He looks at his watch and starts to say it but suddenly stops, realizing my deeper meaning.

"My dad gave this to me," he protests.

"He has wonderful taste," I reply, holding out my palm.

"No," he says. It seems there is still a glimmer of fight left in the Scoobie bean. Tommy gives me a look like that's enough, but it's not. This little skid has now crossed my line.

"You deaf or what?" I ask.

Andy puts his hand over the watch. "You can't have it," he mutters.

"Come on, let's go," Tommy says to me.

"Not just yet." I grab for the timepiece but Andy's grip is firm. He wants to keep his watch. Quaint, really. I wrap my arm around Andy's neck and apply the neck squeeze. As a result, Andy starts turning a peculiar shade of blue.

Just as his face starts going from blue to gray, he surrenders the watch to Tommy. I let him drop to the ground, gulping in air. Tommy hands me the merchandise. I take my time admiring it.

"Very nice. A work of art. Truly."

Then I drop the watch on the gravel and crush it with my foot.

The Andy's face goes from gray to red. He screams, "NO!" and charges at me like a mad bull. I have no choice but to make my hand into a fist and drive it deep into his solar plexus. An elbow to the chin and he sinks at my feet.

"Any last message you want to give him, Tombo?"

"Just one," replies Tommy, who delivers several kicks to Andy's ribs.

At this moment, I look up and notice the spectators scramble off the fence and take off running.

A teacher? The cops?

No. Much worse. A sight from hell.

A very large, pierced and tatted figure has appeared behind Tommy. Shane, he of the killing school. He of the fist, blade and gun. He who is one of the princes of the TMR, a gang so evil, you do not speak the name. They rape, they kill, they burn and destroy, without a blink. I have personally seen the TMR tear a club apart, smashing every person who dared not hide. And from below my upturned table, I watched Shane break a giant bouncer's bones

SKUD

effortlessly, then slice his face. Shane is a demon of terror.

Suddenly our little game is out of place. Who knew the TMR had booked the Cage? No matter. What they want, they get. They can finish working over Scoob if it gives them pleasure.

"Greetings, Shane," I say. "You have some plans for the Cage, I take it?"

He shakes his head.

"Oh," I wonder. "Are you here for the show?"

He shakes his head no again. Then his voice, low, like a lion's growl.

"I'm his backup," saith he.

I'm not sure what I'm hearing. It doesn't make sense. A little laugh escapes from my mouth.

"Scoober's backup? Surely you jest."

I freeze at the sight of him shaking his head. No joke. He means it. Shane, the gang lord, is the Scoob's backup. How can this be? How could this have happened?

"Welcome," I say, oozing hospitality. I drop Scoob's clothes at his feet. "Gotta run," I say, and I take off, Tommy chasing behind. I run very fast.

 I pull myself up. I hurt everywhere. I hate those bugs. I hate everything about them. Why is everything with them smash smash smash?

I look and see who my savior is. Shane. This criminal is my backup? Shane is my backup? The world is filled with miracles.

"You okay?" he asks.

"I'd like to 86 those fleas." I stammer.

"No, you wouldn't," Shane says, his voice low and flat. He says it so you know it's a fact.

I know I couldn't do it. That's why they can just stomp me at will. That's *why* they stomp me at will. Because they can and I can't. But if I could, I would.

He carefully picks up my dad's watch and gazes at it. Then, without a word, holds it out to me.

I finish pulling on my pants and have a look. The glass is shattered, the hands are twisted, hanging like dead fish. It's six-thirty forever.

"Just sentimental value," I say, putting my shirt back on.

"That's worth something," he says. And when I shrug, he adds, "More than you think."

I know he's right. My dad gave me the watch a year before he got sick. On my birthday. "Time is precious," Dad said. Six months later he got sick. I keep wondering if he knew what was coming.

Shane stares at me and his eyes don't have that cold look in them. They almost look soft and watery. He must be wearing contacts or something. I'm starting to wonder what's going with this banger. He's the most feared guy in the universe and he's talking to me, he's being my backup. These are not things I understand.

43

"Some kind of TMR thing coming this way?" I ask.

"I'm out of it."

I'm shocked, I really am. "You quit the TMR?"

He stares at me those big moony eyes. After about a year, he finally says, "No one ever quits."

I nod, pretending I know something about it. He starts to go. "Shane. Thanks for the backup."

He doesn't turn around or say you're welcome or anything. He just keeps going. And I'm standing there pinching myself. Shane, TMR Shane, saved my chickens. Shane, the bloody giant, appeared like Superman and chased the bugs away. Could this be real? Did the gods look down on my poor suffering soul and send me my very own guardian devil?

Once upon a time I had good back-up. I had the best backup in the world.

He'd take it for me, or me for him, whatever kept us alive. Since we were three, four, five.

Mama always had a new guy who'd come home tanked, bust us up. Once, I was twelve, New Guy was slamming my face in the wall, painting the plaster red. My backup picks up Mama's hot iron and presses his butt. It worked. New Guy let me go.

No matter who New Guy was we'd stand up

together. Pay the price together. Be the eyes in back of each other's heads.

We had to. We were brothers.

TOMMY I run and run. Is TMR after us? Every car could be a drive-by, every person passing could be the one with the gun. I shift into Terrorist Counter Measures. I'm probably outnumbered so a precise retreat is required. Stick to high ground for visibility, main streets provide camouflage. I deke from doorway to doorway, avoiding crowds to limit civilian casualties. This method is slow and painstaking but will shield them from the indiscriminate spray of the gang's automatic gunfire.

Finally home is in sight. I wait at the corner, survey the terrain before proceeding. With no opposition sighted, I sprint evasive, in a zigzag pattern. At the door, I turn the key and run up the four floors. No elevator for me, I don't want to get trapped. What if the doors open and the TMR is standing there? I open the stairwell door and peek into the hallway. Clear. Slip down hall, key apartment door and open. Tuck inside, bolt door. Safe.

Soft sound of breathing. Grandma asleep on couch. This is good. This will help. I sit down on chair across from her and watch her chest go up and down. The snoring is soft. Pounding in my heart

SKUD

slows down. Throbbing in head letting up. Watching her releases all pain. Nothing better than watching Grandma sleep. There is no peace like hers. I wish I could go where she goes when she sleeps.

I watch her for an hour, maybe longer. Until all the vibrations have left my body and even my breathing is like hers. Then the phone rings and the spell ends. She wakes up and looks at me.

"You gonna get it?"

I pick up but it's the wrong number. Grandma smiles at me.

"You just get home, Thomas?"

"Yeah, just this minute."

"How was your day in school?"

"Great. I got an A on my biology assignment. And I made the Honor Roll again."

"I'm so proud of you." Her pale blue eyes caress me. "How's your girlfriend, honey?"

I knew she'd ask. She always does. "She's happy. Got the lead in the school play. I bought her flowers."

"That's nice." I help her stand up. Her hips need replacing and she's on the waiting list. She's been waiting two years. The scum weaseling doctors keep people like her at the bottom of the list. But Grandma's an angel. She never complains, never holds a grudge. Grandma is pure goodness.

Then she drops it on me.

"Your mother called."

"So?" I know what's coming.

"She wants to have her visit."

"I'm busy."

"You have to see her, Thomas. Just once a month."

The throbbing starts in my head again.

"Okay. When?"

"Would next Saturday be all right? I could make a little lunch."

"I won't have a stomach for eating."

Grandma gets a sad look. "Just try a little with her. Please, my darling?"

I can't look in her soft, worn-out eyes. I just say, "Sure, Grandma, whatever."

And she takes my hand and kisses it. Then gives me one of her homemade doughnuts. I lick the powder off and then I eat it. They are the best.

 That night I wait for Tommy outside his apartment. I never go up there. I can't stand the reek of the place. I don't appreciate his grandmother's turkey-wattle eyes. I don't like the way her claws are clamped into Tommy or how he bows down to her or the vile things she says about me.

She suspects me of an impure heart. She's full of skud. She doesn't know me. She doesn't know what made me the way I am. She knows nothing about me, yet tells Tomster, my best friend, that I am a

SKUD

negative, that I am wasted potential. She's the wasted one. With age comes dementia. Will this be my father's fate? My fate? To end up a limping corpse with X-ray eyes?

I sit in my GT watching the door, listening to the rock thrashing through my speaker, waiting for Tomster. He does not come so I call him on my cell. The T says hello like he's been doing the smoke.

"C'mon, Sarge, where are you?"

"I fell asleep," he mumbles.

"Well, wake up, let's go!"

"I'm a waste, go without me."

"Sure," I say, and I lean on the horn and chug the music up so the bass is rattling glass and lights start going on up and down the block. I see a window open and Tombo's head sticks out, the phone still to his ear.

"Okay, stop, I'm coming!" he says, and the window closes again.

Finally he joins me and we head over to the Ratchit Room, my favorite club.

Choice DJs, cream lights and sound, prime skrunk and the proprietor never ID's. Tonight some kind of Asian fix is on. Chinese lions are dancing around, a samurai's walking on stilts, and some Kabuki guy is eating fire. The dance floor is sardined as usual but I don't feel like dancing yet. I need Tommy to loosen enough to spill the truth to me. For I suspect my dear friend is holding out on me.

I pull Tombo and his beer into a corner. "Your juicer the Scoob has quality backup."

Tommy shakes his head. I can tell he's rattled. "It makes no sense. I never heard about him and a TMR connection. And that Shane – wasn't he just in a big murder thing? What was he doing with Scoob?"

"Exactly the question that's been plaguing my brain," says I. "Hoped you might shed some light on the subject."

A strobe light starts flashing on Tommy's face. He cringes and covers his eyes. For a second I wonder if he's gonna go into convulsions. "I swear, this is complete news to me, Brad."

I take a long slow sip of my brew. "I thought they taught you about surveillance in the cadets, about evaluating the opposition's resources."

"I did the check on Scoob, I did. There was nothing. It shouldn't have happened."

"But it did," I remind him. "That's a very sad, embarrassing thing."

"I know," Tommy agrees, just as a green-painted guy in a dragon mask ambles over to us, puts his hand to his mouth and breathes fire.

"Do it again," I say, holding out my cigarette. He blows fire and I light my smoke. My digits get a little crisp, but I like the feeling.

"You burned your fingers," Tombo points out.

"Didn't notice," I tell him and get back to topic. "You swear you know nothing about Shane being there?"

SKUD

"Why would I lie? Did you see how he eyed us? Cold, like a butcher ready to cut."

I nod. "He's pure professional. He scopes the size of the major veins and arteries, all in the service of determining the best place to slice."

"He shouldn't be allowed on the streets."

"Bangers at Shane's level own the streets."

Tom shakes his head. "That's anarchy."

"That's balance. It puts fear into you, and peace into him."

Tommy's face goes white and his little scar goes whiter. "Someone should take him down," he says, looking very far away.

This is the Tom I love, the walking time bomb. So quiet, so dangerous. One day I know he'll surprise us all. I pull hard on my beer, killing it. "Everybody thinks you are such an upstanding, well-behaved guy. If they only could see how much more there is to you."

Tommy looks at me, nervous. "Everybody at the Cage saw it today."

"Nah, nah, they saw an MG'd guy doing what was right. Doing his duty. You have nothing to fear."

"I hope you're right."

"I'm always right," I state, and head over to the dance floor.

ANDY I watch Shane exit, still trying to figure out what happened, when I feel this vibration in my pocket. For a second I wonder if Tommy severed an artery when he was kicking me and I'm bleeding to death internally and don't know it. Then I remember my pager's on vibrate mode. It's a wonder Brad didn't find it in my pocket and break that too.

It's a message from my agent. He said he might have an audition for me today. He called an hour ago! I can't believe I've kept him waiting that long. I start for the school pay phone and feel a big pain in my leg. Tommy must have caught my thigh bone with his foot.

I limp across the gravel and finally get to the phone. I dial Preston's number from memory. If you want to make it as an actor, you have to memorize your agent's number and phone her or him once a day, just to say hello. Even if you're just talking to their voice mail. You have to make sure they're always thinking of you. Out of sight, out of mind, the saying goes. So you call your agent a lot. Does this make me a pain in the ass? Yes. But consider Matt Damon, Keanu Reeves, Leo DiCaprio. All of them are pains in the ass. They all phone their agents nine to fifteen times a day. If you don't push, you get nowhere. And once you're somewhere, everybody expects you to be a hemorrhoid. If you're not, you have no status. So I do what I have to. Push, push, push! Call, call, call!

51

SKUD

The phone rings. The secretary answers. "Young Talent Inc."

"Hi, Sally, how are you?" I say, turning the charm meter way up. Another thing I've learned. Sally is the receptionist. Always, always, always know the receptionist's name. Always, always kowtow the receptionist. They move very quickly up the food chain. I have been with Young Talent Inc. for ten months. Two receptionists have already left to be associate producers with major players. The receptionists are at least as important as their bosses. Besides, they're usually younger, so they'll be around longer.

"Andy? I'm fine, thanks. And you?"

"Fantastic," I say, acting to the hilt, since every bone in me is aching, "and I'm feeling a million times better just hearing your voice on the phone."

"He's looking for you," she says. "Hold on."

My mouth is watering, my blood is pumping hard. She's actually putting me through to Preston. The real Preston. Not a message. Not his voice mail. This is the first time in six months – maybe eight – that I've actually talked to him. The air is thin when your agent puts down everything just to pass words with you.

All my aches and pains seem far away. Even the Muzak they play on hold sounds beautiful. It's Nirvana played slow and romantic with strings. I'm humming along.

Sally gets back on the blower. "Sorry, Andy, he's tied up on a call to L.A. I know it's late, but Preston wants you to get over to the Gastown Workshop for a seven o'clock audition. It's an action feature called Rocco's Last Hit."

I admit I'm disappointed that I've missed the great man again. But now I have to play for time.

"Today? Are they really going this late?" I say, trying to buy some time to recover from my injuries. "Wouldn't it be better for me to go tomorrow?

"Nope, this is it," she says. "Your only shot."

So I have no choice. "I'm there. What part am I reading for?"

"Punk," she says.

"Punk? Does it say anything else?"

"No, just 'Punk.'"

"Nothing about who he is, or what he is?"

I hear a little sigh on the other end, like I'm overstepping.

"No, Andy. It just says 'Punk.' Are you going or not?"

"Yeah, I'm going, I'm going."

"You're an angel," she says, and *click*.

I look at my watch. And remember it's smashed. I peer down the empty hallway. The old clock says quarter to six. Not good. I phone home. My mom answers.

"Andy? Where are you?"

"At school. I got tied up on a special project."

For a second I worry that she's gonna wonder about the nature of this project. But she's pushing ahead.

SKUD

"Dinner's almost served."

"Problem, Mom. I got something I gotta do."

"I know. Another audition."

Skud. She knows. I got the beeper so the agency's calls wouldn't funnel home. My luck, they left a message there too.

"It'll be quick and I'll come straight home," I tell her.

"Don't waste your time on garbage, Andy."

"It's not, Mom, I swear it. My agent said this movie's about saving the whales. It's about Greenpeace."

I can almost hear her considering my fabrication. Understand, there's a good reason for me to lie. My mom is a person who isn't comfortable with the world. In fact, she hates it. She believes that five companies control all the newspapers and television stations and movie companies and they're hypnotizing the population into a buy-buy-buy mentality.

Once, when I was six, she gave away our TV. My dad was cool because he could watch the ball games in the sports bar. But my little body went into shock. Really. I started hyperventilating all the time, couldn't sleep, couldn't eat. For a week my temper tantrums could be heard through the whole neighborhood. Finally the police knocked on the door. Somebody complained, thinking somebody was being tortured. My parents explained but the cops didn't comprehend. Why would any sane person throw out their television set? A social worker came for a visit and my mother was completely outraged. Now the government is putting the family under investigation for turning off the TV. My mom explained that she thought the cathode was bad for my brain, but the social worker just looked at her funny. Needless to say, we got a new TV the next day.

Mom may have lost the battle, but the war is still on.

"So you're telling me this is a Greenpeace movie?" She asks me.

"That's right, Mom. They see this film as a great opportunity to promote environmentalism."

"What's the part?"

"A student activist. I'm really pumped. Finally a role with some social responsibility."

"Somehow I have difficulty believing a movie called Rocco's Last Hit has a lot of whales in it," she says.

"This could be a real break, Mom."

"You can bullshit me if you want, Andy. Just don't bullshit yourself. See you whenever you get home."

She hangs up and I limp over to the bus stop. You'd think somebody on mood control pills would be a little less on the ball. She doesn't get the acting thing at all. It's like I'm hanging with the enemy. She always asks me how movies help humanity. Well, I'm human, right? That means I'm humanity, okay? So if I make it in Hollywood, I'm giving humanity a big boost.

SKUD

And all this can happen if the bus ever gets here. You see, this is Vancouver, where the clouds never part and the buses never come. I could probably walk there faster – that is, if I could walk right now. First good part that pays some bucks, I'm buying some wheels. First, of course, I have to learn to drive. Okay, shut up, so I don't have my license. She wouldn't let me. Said there's already too many drivers on the road and nobody under the age of eighteen is mature enough to be behind the wheel of a pollution machine. Truth is, she's just petrified I'll get mangled and she'll be completely alone. I'll buy something simple, like an old Corvette. And if I go big, a Porsche. No matter how rich I get, I'll never spend more than fifty or sixty thousand on a car. Any more than that would be a waste of money. And no more than three cars at a time. I wouldn't want to be pretentious. And could you imagine the cost of insurance?

I see my reflection in the glass of the bus shelter. One black eye. One puffy lip. Maybe my mom is right. This audition is a waste of time. My face looks like Spam. I'm in no shape to do this thing. But I have to.

I stop arguing with myself because, miraculously, the bus arrives. I'm on my way.

The Gastown Workshop is an old brick building on an old brick street filled with tourists taking snapshots of each other in front of a whistling clock. I push through somebody's Kodak moment and go inside. Take the ancient elevator up to the third floor. The doors open and I see this one big dude swing his arm.

"You want it? Here, die, suck!" he yells.

I lurch back in the elevator, just in case I'm in the wrong place and he's armed. But no bullets come.

I am in the right place. It's like an embarrassing Halloween party where everybody came in the same costume. The hallway's filled with gangbangers. All different colors and dos, it's like tough-guy paradise.

All these reputed bangers have "sides" in their hands. They're practicing lines from the script. One brutal dude, with his head shaved into a big X, is pressing something on his arm. For a second I think he's shooting up. But then I see him peel a paper off the spot. It's a press-on tattoo.

Next to me is this guy with gold chains and black satin, looking pretty spooky. Then I see it's Nathan, this roach I bump into so much at auditions, he thinks we're friends.

"I'll rip your heart out with my teeth," he growls at me. I don't buy it, particularly since I saw him at an audition last week, trying out for the part of a gay waiter. He loses the sneer and asks, "How do I look, Andy?"

"Great, Nathan, scary stuff."

He shakes his head. "I can't believe it. I forgot the tooth!" He reaches in his pocket, pulls out this shiny thing and pushes it on his incisor. It's a fake gold cap with a diamond in the middle. He smiles at me, showing off his new mouth.

SKUD

"Good idea, huh? I got it down in Seattle."

"Dazzling," I say, and I head over to the casting assistant to give her my name. She checks me off, gives me some sides, and says it won't be much of a wait. All these other guys have slots after me. They came early to read the script, and came prepared.

I can't believe Sally didn't tell me I was supposed to dress up for this thing. Every single guy here was told by his agent to come with the criminal look – every guy except me. So here I am, the beat-up geeky schoolboy, instead of the tough JD. I am such a loser.

I slump down on the floor next to this all black leather guy and have a look at the lines. There's not much to learn.

INT. ROCCO'S PLACE – NIGHT

A young-looking PUNK, all pills and attitude, shuffles in. Rocco nonchalantly looks up.

                    ROCCO
              Did you bring it?

                    PUNK
         Yeah.

He hands Rocco some money.

                    ROCCO
              Is that everything?

                    PUNK
         Yeah.

                    ROCCO
         I don't think so. I think you're short.

The Punk lifts an eyebrow.

                    PUNK
         Yeah?

                    ROCCO
         You're way short, sucker.

In a flash, Rocco's Magnum is out and he pumps
three shells into the Punk's chest. The Punk gives
Rocco a puzzled look and falls over.

                    ROCCO
         I hate short people.

         CLOSE ON – BLOOD

The puddle under the Punk grows and grows, covering the entire floor in red and we
                                        CUT TO:

    That's as much of the script as they gave me. Like
Sally said, the part I'm going for, along with everybody else, is the Punk, who has three lines, which,

SKUD

believe it or not, is very good. It's an actual speaking part, so it pays lots. And it's a whole scene with the star. And there's not a lot to memorize.

I limp over to the washroom to see if I can pull myself together. I close the door behind me and lock it. The place stinks of bacterial cleanser. Maybe that's a good thing, the fumes can sterilize my cuts.

I look like scuzz, I feel like scuzz. I can fake my way through it as well as anybody else, but I don't have a prayer. But I know I have to do it. Because the show must go on.

No matter how sick or bent out of shape they might be, real stars never say die. When Jackie Chan breaks his arm during a stunt, does he quit? No chance. They patch him up and he jumps off the next building. When Tom Cruise was shooting M.I.2, you think he cried and went home when he threw his back? No. Actors Act. That is our job. That is what we do. That is how you make it.

I splash some water on my face and glare at myself. "Yeah. Yeah. Yeah?" I say, trying to get inside this character. Think, Andy. You almost just got killed. Punk does get killed. So you have a lot in common. I use the emotional memory technique to locate that connection. I take a deep breath and feel a sudden pain in my rib where Tommy booted me. This is good. This is how you call up the memories.

I am the Punk. I am the Punk. I am the Punk.

I push my nose right into the mirror. "Yeah," I say. "Yeah." Then I recall Rocco's last words to me.

"Yeah?" I say and breathe deep, feeling the pain in my ribs and imagine it's Rocco's bullets hitting me. I sink to my knees, the blood pouring out. I fall on the bathroom tiles and die.

Suddenly I hear the door open. I quickly get up and head for the door as a fake thug in a muscle shirt ambles in. That's when I hear them calling my name.

I exhale very slowly a bunch of times, settling my nerves. And I shuffle into the room, just like the punk in the script.

The room is small. Inside is a table with actors' headshots and resumes piled on it. Three people are behind the table. A guy, twenty or so, is standing by a video camera. A tall girl with short black hair and eyebrow rings is sitting near him. Across from all of them is a chair that's sitting by a black screen.

I'm feeling all gloom and doom but I try not to show it.

"Hello, Andy," this woman in a gold dress says to me. "I'm Rita, the casting agent. This is Dean, the director/producer and Morgan, the producer/writer."

These two guys who look exactly the same wave their hands. They're both around thirty, and are twins, I presume. They have little chin beards and narrow sideburns and are wearing denim jeans and jackets. The only difference: Dean has on a white T-shirt and Morgan is wearing a black T-shirt.

"Who does your make-up?" asks Rita.

This throws me a little. When we put on the Wizard of Oz, my drama teacher did the make-up. I

61

SKUD

was a very convincing Cowardly Lion, but somehow I'm not sure that information will help me get the part of a small-time drug dealer.

"Truth is, it's not make-up," I say.

Dean leans in for a closer look. "He's right, it's the real thing."

They all nod their heads. I can't tell if they're impressed or if they think I'm the world's biggest wanker. Dean and Morgan tug on their little beards. Then Dean says, "Any time you're ready."

I limp over to the chair and I hear Morgan whisper. "He's got the walk."

From his tone I assume he's mocking my limp but I can't stop now, I can't let that kind of negativity rattle me. Focus is everything. No matter how they try to throw you, good actors play through it. That's what we do. The tall girl with the short black hair nods to me.

"Hi, I'll be reading with you today," she says. She doesn't look much like I imagined Rocco, but the camera's on me, not her.

"Did you bring it?" she asks in this very high voice. She's definitely not my idea of Rocco.

"Yeah," I reply, trying to sound a little stoned like the guy in the script.

"Is that everything?" she says, with this tired voice. I guess this is the two hundredth time she's read the lines today.

"Yeah," I reply, exactly as written in the script by the twin sitting across from me.

"I don't think so. I think you're short," she says in a total monotone. Where do they find these people to read?

"Yeah?" I go, trying to put a little lilt on the question. I play it like I have no idea that anything is wrong, that I'm relaxed from the dope and all is well in the world.

Then *BOOM!* Dean smacks his open palm on the table. I practically jump out of my skin. I look up startled, my eyes bugged open.

Dean and Morgan both laugh.

"Good, surprise. Good. You're dead!" says Dean.

"Thanks very much," says Rita. "We'll let your agent know."

That's it. The whole thing.

"Thank you," I say, and I limp back out the door. Did they like me? I have no idea. In fact, they probably hated me. Will they cast me? Dream on.

As soon as I'm out the door, Nathan's all over me.

"How did it go?"

I shrug. "All right, I guess."

"You were in there a long time."

"Oh, come on," I say. "It took about three seconds. I read the scene and left."

"They let you read the whole scene? That's amazing!"

"There's like four lines in the scene. It's no big whoop."

"Did they like your look?"

"I don't know."

SKUD

Nathan groans. "I knew it, the minute you walked in. They don't want fake, they want real. You're real. They must love that."

I don't say anything. I'm praying he's right, but no point getting your hopes up.

"Only one thing to do," Nathan says, and he faces the wall and bangs his face in it. Then he turns back to me. "Is it bleeding?"

"Is what bleeding?"

"My nose. It usually bleeds easy. Better give it another shot." He boings his nose into the wall again. "Anything?"

I shake my head.

"Nathan Levinsky." The casting assistant calls out his name. Now it's his turn and he's panicking. He doesn't want to go in there if he's not bleeding. It's the only way to top my bruises.

"Coming!" Nathan yells back and starts bashing his face in the wall again.

I hop in the elevator and push the button down.

It's amazing, really. Some people will do anything to get a part.

 I slip my GT into the driveway about 2 A.M. Look up. Moon's a sliver. I know it's cold because I can see my breath. I take off my jacket and throw it on the hood. Tonight I don't feel my body. I feel all mind. Is it the booze? No. Tonight my brain is beyond all fixes because somehow the world has shifted. Things are not like they seemed.

Scoob's a puzzle. An obvious tomato, a free squash, a nothing. First he MG's Tommy, stealing the skrunk of my poor compadre's dreams. Then, when hell comes to pay, Scoob turns out to be joined at the hip to Shane, the Terror of all Mankind.

Why does this bother me? Because I work for what I am. I spend hours in gym sculpting what I am. And this one, this Scoob, is a nose in a book, a poser on a stage, a nothingness. I am the muscle. Why doesn't Shane call on me? Is it the brains the TMR are after? And if it's brains they admire, why have I let my own brain cells rot?

A light goes on in the house. The door opens. Out comes father of mine, puffing on a cigarillo. No surprise he's up and around. He doesn't sleep much.

"Hey, Sonny, catching the night air?

Many fathers who are less than prime rag into their offspring for coming home late. Not my good old dad. Dad of mine does not worry about bedtime. There's never but one thing on his mind.

"How was practice today?" asks he, handing me a cigarillo. I take it, not because I like chewing on the plastic tip, but out of comradely spirit. And so we sit on my car hood, blowing cigarillo clouds at the sliver moon.

"Practice was good," says I, and for some reason,

SKUD

the worried face of my red-nosed coach flashes before my eyes.

"I did some calculations, Bradley," he says, puffing a perfect ring around the North Star. "Your plus/minus is two plus."

"This is good," says I. For this to be true, every time I step on ice, my team is ahead. Rare is the goal scored against us while I play. More are the goals we score when I stalk the ice. Scouts will hear this. They will want to see more of me. But dear Dad disagrees.

"Two plus is not four plus." Daddy Mine says. "Four plus is an average that gets junior league contracts. Two plus gets you dick." He sucks large on the cigarillo, breathes in the smoke and blows it out his nostrils.

"Then I'll do better," say I.

"Much better is what you'll do. You weren't born with greatness. You were born a lump of shit. But I never cursed Our Maker. I accepted what I was given and molded it. I took your miniscule potential, poured in all my time, money and knowledge, and turned you into a hockey machine. But all the skill I gave you is zero unless you burn a hole in your ass.

I nod. I know he's right. Ideas are nothing. Hope is nothing. Work is everything. Everything that I am is because of him.

I watch him suck deep on the cigarillo. And I consider what a generous person he is. To focus his whole life, his whole being on one thing. Me. I am a very lucky person.

"Dad," I say, "on ice, I see it all. I do not check the opponent just for the pleasure of crushing his bones. I smash him because I can see he will take the next pass that will be shot at the head of our goalie. My eyes see everything. On ice I have vision, but on land, it's not the same. I thought I could anticipate every shot coming my way. But sometimes I miss."

"Then you'll always be an amateur," he says, stubbing out his smoke. "You have to learn to dominate twenty-four hours a day. You can't toggle switch that kind of mental control. If it's not always on, you're out."

Mental control. Am I losing brain matter? Mr. Gee claims the pills cause mood swings, affect concentration.

No. Not my pills.

Father Mine peers at my face. "You're drifting. Where is your mind?"

This kind of doubt he cannot hear. So I give him another kind of doubt.

"At school. Mr. Gee suggested I read more books to exercise my mind. He thinks it would help build back the synapses from all those head concussions."

A darkness crosses his brow. "Who trains you? Mr. Gee or me?"

"Only you. Mr. Gee is nothing."

"Are you suddenly telling me you are afraid of taking a check?"

"I take them and give them, Dad. It's what I do. I'm just telling you about Mr. Gee and books."

SKUD

"Read all you want, Bradley. But rest assured, no scout will ever ask you if you read Shakespeare. You want focus?"

"Yes," I say.

"Then focus on this. In hockey, it's all about the team, not one man. In life, it's all about one man, you. Not the team. Remember that and you'll always win, on and off the ice."

Then he slaps me. "Are you listening?"

"I heard every word," say I, my cheek burning.

"Good," he says and nods. "I love you, son."

I like when he says that. I watch him go into the house and I look back up at the sky. I can't see the moon anymore. There's a thin cloud layer covering the whole sky. Must have misted over so quick, I didn't see it happen.

 Morning light against my eyelids. I stare at the back of them like a movie screen. I can see corpuscles, like little worms, floating. If I try not to look, I see them. Move my eye, they dart away.

My grandma believes God is always watching us. She's told me that since I was a kid. Every Sunday she goes to church and most of the time I go with her. Most people suspect I go because the Commander goes too. He has told us that good officers are devout, and even if they are not, they still pay their respects to a Higher Power.

What no one knows is that I don't go to brown nose the Commander. I could never tell anybody this, because I know what they'd think and I have an image to protect. I'm a clear-thinking, responsible, logical person who will soon go to flight school and become an officer. This person that I am to the world could never reveal the true reason I go to church. I go because I want Him to touch me. I sing the psalms and say the prayers, waiting for His Grace. But I never get it, ever. I keep going back because I know He's there. At times like this, times like now, I can feel His eyes on me.

God, I know you can see me. I can feel you watching me, like I watch the corpuscles. Why don't you reach down and touch my stomach and fill me with light?

Every morning this is my prayer. Every morning God ignores me.

I smell bacon. I smell frying eggs. I smell toast. I wish I didn't have to eat food.

I can feel the angel, locked in this prison of my skin and bone, my body a shell for this heavenly being. My life is a mistake. I should be flying with wings through the universe. Instead I slog in the mud down here.

I was shut out by God an eon ago. Thrown out of heaven, with the dark angels, forever cursed to lose the Light. Falling, falling, slammed into a baby

SKUD

being pulled out of a womb and trapped in its little bones.

My body's a punishment for sins I can't even remember. I keep growing but the force inside me, it tears me apart. The headaches, the chills, the strangeness I'm always feeling, the strangeness I always hide. It's because we keep missing, Me and God, both our eyes moving to try and see each other but we float away.

Why can't I go back to Him? My skin pure light, my hair blazing like the sun. Held in His embrace forever. Again. When will God bring me home?

When a pilot bails in the wilderness, he sets up signal fires, lights flares to call the rescue team. His homing device sends signals to say where he is. F-16 pilots are valuable, highly trained specialists. The air force never leaves them stranded. And if they crash land dead, they're brought back for a hero's burial.

Why won't You bring me back? Why have You left me stranded?

ANDY I'm on the way to school when my beeper goes off. It's my agent. My stomach starts fluttering. I don't want to get excited, but it's hard to stop.

Agents phoning you first thing in the morning is always a good sign. It's even better when they start calling you on the weekends, or from their villa in Mexico when they're on holiday. When that happens, you are made. Your agent can't relax without connecting with you all the time. Why? Because you are no longer mere human. You are a star. You are their pay check. So you can understand my agitation. This call is coming before 9 A.M. This call is real.

Being without a cell due to lack of funds, I duck into a smashed-up phone booth. The phone, unfortunately, is missing. Somebody tore it off the cable when they trashed it. I used to think the ongoing destruction of pay phones was the work of disgruntled youth. But my mom believes the cell phone companies are responsible. It's a conspiracy to force everybody to go wireless. My mom might be a paranoid mess, but on this one, I'm onside. I don't know any kids who waste pay phones. We need them too bad.

I run up to a corner store and ask the owner if I can use his phone. He looks up from the licorice twists like I'm total psycho whack. His brown eyes go real big like I'm about to knock over the store.

"Private phone," he says.

"I'll give you a buck for one local call," I offer. He takes the dollar and hands me the phone. I punch in Preston's number in a flash. It rings once, twice, and then I hear Sally's voice.

"Young Talent Inc."

"Hi, Sally, it's Andy – "

"Hang on, Andy, he wants to talk to you."

And she puts me on hold. I think I heard her

SKUD

right. He wants to talk with me. Preston wants to talk with Andy. Him with me. I must be dreaming.

And then I hear the great man's voice.

"Hey, Andy, good work yesterday!" I can't believe that Preston, my agent, is giving me direct feedback. Like I'm one of his stars.

"Thanks, Preston. Did they like me?"

"Like you? They loved you! They put you on the short list!"

I can't breathe. I'm trying to get air inside but it's not going in.

"How many are on the short list?" I can't help asking.

"Lots. But that's not the point, Andy. Do you know who those two guys were?"

"The twins? The director/producer/writer guys?"

"Those aren't just guys, kid. They are Double A List. Those are the Brothers Qualm. They're the hottest thing in L.A. Their last movie, The Naked Corpse, grossed two hundred million. Domestic."

I'm in awe. I only saw that picture nine times. It's Tarantino meets Woo meets Spielberg. I can't believe I was in the same room with them and didn't realize it.

"They're geniuses," I say. "I love them! Do I get a call-back?"

"They said they adored your look, Andy," says Preston. Then he asks, "What'd you do to your look?"

"Nothing much. I was a little worse for wear."

"Well, it'll take more than a look to get the part. These guys want real. They're looking for somebody who they can totally believe as a doped-out gang-banger. They love your physical being but they need convincing on the acting side."

My heart sinks. They didn't like my acting.

"I'm screwed, huh?"

"No, Andy, no," says Preston. "You just need an acting coach. Somebody to help you with your believability. Your verisimilitude."

"There's only three lines," I say.

"That's changing. They told me they're adding to the part."

"This is incredible." I'm completely in shock.

"This could be your break, Andy. Knock 'em dead."

"When's the call-back?" I stammer.

"Next week or so. I'll let you know when I get the time."

He hangs up and I'm completely numb. The shopkeeper takes the phone from my hand and hangs it up.

The store suddenly doesn't look grungy anymore. The brown bananas have a golden tint, the row of beef jerky has a silver aura, the dust on the oatmeal boxes is glowing. Even the withered shopkeeper's bloodshot eyes are glistening. I stumble out into the blazing sunlight and it blinds me like a spotlight's on me and the whole world is giving me a standing O.

I'm called back. Me. By the Brothers Qualm.

73

SKUD

BRAD

Scoober. Every time the blackness starts rolling over me, I see his face. Soft, simple, filled with fear.

But then another face appears behind him. Shane. And now Andy's face shifts. His eyes turn red, and his lips curl, showing his teeth, all steel and gold, filed into fangs. And then he bites.

Scoober. A demon in disguise. I look where he's bitten me. Red pits of acne scars across my back and shoulders. I look down at my chest. My pecs are swelling...turning round and soft. Nooooo!

And then I wake up. Sweating ice.

After no sleep, I'm in the can, washing my face, checking my perfect skin and pecs when Mother Mine hands me my morning power drink.

"Drink up, baby. You got a big practice today."

Mother of mine is dressed to the nines, her skirt short and her heels high. She is beauty itself, once runner-up to Miss Vancouver.

"How's my hair, honey?" she asks as I gulp down the protein fix.

"Blonde," I reply. "Nice."

She smiles. "You really like it?"

I smile back. "You're a dish."

She frowns. "I look old."

"No. You're prime."

Her lips turn up again. "You are so sweet," says she, takes the empty glass and leaves me there at the sink, watching the water swirl down the drain hole.

Watching it flow out of the tap and go down the hole, an idea presents itself. Surrender.

I run out to the GT and floor it to the school. I run stop signs and a red light or two. I have to catch Scoob before he goes into class. I get to school and buzz around the block, hoping to spot him.

But he's nowhere. No Andy in the front, no Andy in the back. Could I have missed him? I pull up behind the school and scan the playing field. Nothing. I look at the sky for a second and something catches my eye. Someone's on the roof. Someone who resembles the Scoob, just standing there, talking to himself. It's him.

I park and dash into the building. Hammer up the stairs, then I find the janitor's stairwell that takes you to the roof. It's nice up here, nicer than you'd expect. In front of me is the Andy himself, chanting some weird jibberish. It must be a martial arts meditation, maybe even some kind of communion with darkness. More and more I realize this Scoob is no Scoob. He's a force that must be reckoned with.

"Hey, Andy!" I call out. He jumps in the air, utterly taken by surprise. Then he turns and eyes me like I'm some kind of wild animal come to tear his throat out.

"Andy?" He's surprised that I'm addressing him by his given name.

"Yes, I speak your true name. I come in peace."

I take a careful step toward him. He takes a careful step back. Clearly we have a trust problem here.

75

I continue. "I just wanted to say sorry for all that. Sincere and heartfelt apologies."

He shakes his head. "You came up here to say you're sorry?"

I sigh with heavy heart. "These things happen, you know. It's the times, the way of the world. Misunderstandings, arguments, conflict. Unfortunate. But I've had a bad night's sleep, thinking long and hard about the sad events of yesterday."

He's listening. Half the battle. I play my next card. "Are you carrying the watch?"

He looks at me, not understanding. "What about it?"

I smile beneficently at him. "The repair is mine."

"Pass," is all that comes from his lips. And so I must work harder to win his affection.

"Andy, I got a trifle pumped up. The same thing happens to me when I'm skating. A puck or a stick in my face and click! Smash a jaw, break a watch. Nez pa?"

"Slightly," he replies, his face scowly, almost Shane-like.

"I'm saying it wasn't me who tormented you, Andrew, it was my training. I'm just built that way. Once the button is pushed, it can't be reversed. I regret that the button was pressed, but it happened, what's done is done. Now I come to you, head bowed, filled with remorse and apology. Please. Let me examine the damaged goods."

The school bell rings but neither of us even

flinches as the air grows still. I watch him. Then I see his hand move. It goes into his pocket. For a moment I freeze. I think he's going for a weapon. He catches the look on my face and smiles.

He pulls out the smashed watch.

"May I?" I ask with pure graciousness.

He ponders my face, my hand. He's mastered the Shane face, inscrutable. How long have those two been running? Then, almost like an afterthought, he places the wounded timepiece in my palm. I admire its golden case, its delicate hands. And I shake my head sadly.

"It's beautiful. It's old. Is it rare?"

Scoober is quiet for a moment. Then he softly says, "It meant something to me."

I nod, oozing with sympathy. "From your dead dad, isn't it?"

"Correct."

"Let me get this fixed."

He hardens. "No."

I put more weight into the issue. "It was collateral damage. I'll fix it. It's the very least I can do."

"I don't think so," he replies.

As I feared, Scoob is no easy push. He's filled with curves and twists that never meet the eye. But I stay calm. I keep my grace. A seagull swoops down a few feet from me. I think about how it can swallow a two-pound trout whole. The bird is close enough to kick. I resist the urge to bust off its head, spill its stinking guts all over this putrid asphalt roof. I look mournfully at Scoobie Doo Doo.

SKUD

"Breaking gifts from dead fathers is shameful. I'm ashamed. Let me make penance. Please."

He ponders. He thinks. He weighs. Then he nods. "Okay."

The weight lifts. I smile. "Thank you, Andy. You don't know how much this means to me. You see, I want friendship."

Scoob eyes me like he's staring at a cobra. "I don't think so."

I give him the sheepish look of a dog that's been caught messing the rug. "I understand your hesitation. We can take it slow."

He has this neutral look on his face. I can't tell if he's on side or not.

"Just give me a chance, okay?" I say.

Andy breathes. I'd pay hard cash to know the thoughts banging in his skull. Then he shrugs.

"Okay."

The weight lifts. The tension flees. Andy picks up his pack and moves toward the door.

"So tell me," I ask, with pure nonchalance, nary a quiver in my brow. "How many moons you been souling with Shane?"

He whirls at me, his hairs bristling. "Is that what this is all about?"

I keep underestimating this knight. So I do some fancy repair work. "No, Andy, I'm just making chitty chat. Breaking the ice."

"Sure," he says, stepping into the dingy stairwell.

"So how long?" I ask again.

"Long enough." I'm not comforted by his answers.

"Have you done battle with him before?" I ask. He pauses. I watch another seagull land on the roof. He breathes. Deep. Then he looks into my eyes.

"Whenever necessary," he says, unsettling me many times more.

"Tell me," I ask, for this is the question that's been plaguing my sleep. "Is he vengeful?"

Andy stares at me. "As in, is he going to cut the bones out of your hands?"

"For example," I reply, and the queasiness is growing inside me. He gives me a look that can only be termed contemptuous.

"You'll have to ask Shane that yourself," he says. "Then again, you could just cut your hands off and save him the trouble."

I laugh. Humor. Scoob is a man of many talents.

"Any time you need backup, Andy, let me know. I'm right behind you. I sincerely mean that."

"Thanks." He starts to go.

"And Andy…" says I. "I'll have your dad's watch for you ASAP."

He nods, not sure whether he believes me, and heads off to class. I look at the broken thing and feel the urge to toss it into the garbage. But no, this trinket is my ticket to freedom.

SKUD

ANDY I can't believe the day I'm having. First Preston, then this thing with Brad. I feel like the whole world has shifted and I'm someone else. I walked late into class and Mr. Tweed didn't even blink. He just kept writing equations on the board. Am I totally whack? After class, I go in the hallway, and it's all, "Hi, Andy!" "How goes it, Andy?" "Nice shirt, Andy!" It doesn't take a year for me to figure that this is the reaction to my having been saved by Shane. Even Mr. Tweed is scared of me now. After the ninetieth kid pays respect to me by my locker, I'm starting to chuckle. I could learn to like this.

Then my dream totally comes true. Sheila. I can see her spot me down the hallway, coming straight toward me. Can this be real? She looks so sweet, strolling to me. Her hair cut short, big earrings dangling on her perfect little ears. I'm all smiles.

Finally she arrives.

"Hey, Sheila," I say. But she's not smiling.

"Are you demented or what?"

I want to say something clever and sexy but all that comes out is, "Huh?"

She shakes her beautiful head. "I heard about yesterday. What kind of moron are you, doing Wrestlemania in the Cage? What is this barbarian skud?"

"I didn't have a choice," I tell her, feeling completely bushwhacked.

"You always have a choice." She stomps off.

For a second I feel lousy, but then as I watch her go, the message hits home. She likes me. She cares. Things just keep getting better.

I spent the whole day looking for Shane at school, but I didn't track him down until I was about two blocks from my house. I cut through the park, the way I always do. I'm passing the monkey bars, contemplating how to hide my war wounds from my mother. She was out by the time I got home last night, but I can't avoid her forever.

Then I hear a voice.

"Hey."

I turn and there he is, sitting on a swing, blowing some smoke. I smile.

"Shane! What're you doing here?"

"I'm just here."

He's just here? In this park, the park I cut through every day? I don't want to even think about what this means. Fact is, I'm just happy to see him.

"I want to thank you, man."

Shane lifts an eyebrow. "Why?"

"Brad came to me. He wants to fix my dad's watch."

Shane takes a deep drag of his smoke and blows it out. "Why do you think?"

I shrug. "Fear, I think."

"He fears you?"

I smile. "No, you."

He doesn't blink. "Oh, yeah?"

SKUD

A cold chill stabs through me. I am standing here, defenseless, casually conversing with Pure Evil. Miss Post's little body flying down the stairs flashes before my eyes. Suddenly I'm taking a quick glance around the park, viewing escape routes. Am I crazy? There is no escape. My only hope is recruitment.

"Have you ever heard of the Qualm twins?" I ask him.

"No," Shane replies. "Are they a problem?

"No, no!" I quickly say. "They're the brothers who made The Naked Corpse."

Shane nods. "I saw that like five times."

"So my agent phoned."

"Agent? For what?"

"For TV, movies, commercials. I'm up for a part. With the Brothers Qualm."

"Gro," Shane says, showing his approval with one little nod of his head. Then I drop it on him.

"I play a gangbanger."

"You?"

"It's the truth. They think I have the look."

Shane chuckles. "No, you don't."

This kind of support doesn't help my confidence. "Don't spill to the producers. If I score, it's a thousand bucks a day, minimum. Right now it's only one day, but they're beefing up the part. I could end up getting five days, maybe ten."

Shane suddenly gets very interested. "Who do you have to waste?"

"Nobody," I say. "I act. But first I have to score

the part." Then I look at him and decide he's ready for the ten-thousand-dollar question. "Will you help?"

Shane looks at me like I'm whack. "I can't act."

"No, no. Me. You coach me. Make me real. Give me authenticity."

He shakes his head and says in that spooky growl of his, "Not possible."

I breathe, then mimic that slumped look of his, the heavy eyelids. And then I parrot his voice.

"Not possible," I say, sounding almost like Shane. He laughs.

"Now that's gimp. You sound like that, you'll get stomped."

"That's why I need you. You gotta teach me."

"Teach you what?"

I'm trying hard to make him understand me. "The works. What you do."

Then I notice this growing darkness falling over his face. His eyes narrow in that way they narrow on a gun sight.

"Are you a rat?" He mutters.

The flight or fight response kicks in and I'm feeling like flight is in order. But I stand my ground.

"No, Shane, I swear it. I'm into research. Research only."

He gives me a disappointed look. "I told you. I'm not doing crime."

"Then just teach me the Thing."

SKUD

His eyelid starts to get twitchy. "What is the Thing?"

"The no fear," I tell him. "The death eyes. The you-who-never-gets-messed-with."

"You think I have this?"

"That's what you are. Totally. Either you were born that way or you learned it."

"Learned what?"

"Everything," I tell him. "It's in whatever you do. How you stand up for yourself. The way you strike fear in people."

"You just do it," he shrugs.

"That's it. That's what I can't do. It. I need the Qualm Brothers to look at me the way people look at you."

He leans over me so his hulking frame is putting me in a lunar eclipse.

"No, you don't," he says, fingering his bald head, leaving red lines where he scratches.

"Yes, I do," I say, but he just walks away. Gone. And I've got less than a week to learn It.

 He says I have this. The Thing. The It.

What I truly have he doesn't know. What I truly have is a hole. A ripped, deep hole. Is this what he wants? Is this what I should give him?

Once, I was two. Me and another. Once two is gone, you are one.

One means no eyes behind you. One means something was torn away.

This is what I have. Nothing.

I come home, put in the key and stop. Voices are coming from inside. I remember. Today is Saturday Next. Inside is the woman who calls herself my mother. I can hear every word.

I hear Grandma talking, her voice calm like a lake with no wind. "He never said the money was for you."

I hear my mother speak. "I want what's coming to me." I press my palms against the door, Number 308, pushing against it, trying to hold back the flood inside me.

"The money he sends is for Thomas."

"The money's mine too."

I open the lock. I walk in. Mother looks at me and smiles.

"Hi, baby." She holds out her arms. I don't move from the door. I just nod hello. Her smile fades, arms drop. She sits down. "How have you been, Tommy?"

"Okay." I lick the sugar off one of Grandma's doughnuts. Grandma tries to smile but it's not working. She looks sad.

SKUD

I don't feel sad. I feel nothing.

"I miss you, baby."

My laser eyes trace her. "No, you just miss the support payments."

I can see the heat rising in her. Just like the old days. She's wishing she had the strap in her hand, ready to put it on me. But there's no strap anymore. They took that away from her and placed me with Grandma. Now if she strapped me, I'd strap her back. I'd teach her how not to sit anymore. Her turn to learn the things she taught me.

Her face goes sad, like the sorrowful clown at the circus. Used to be, after the strap, she'd get the sorry face and cry and hold me, say how bad she felt, that it would never happen again. And it didn't, not for a day or two. Now she just thinks the strap and the sorry face comes up.

"How are things with the cadets?"

"I'm a sergeant now. They're making me a lieutenant soon."

"You still hoping to join the air force next year?"

"It's not hope, it's fact. I'm going straight into flight school to learn how to fly F-16s."

"You'd look good up there, in the air."

Far from you, I'm thinking. So high, so fast, so far away, you'll never touch me. And after my next birthday, no more of these monthly visits. Once I turn eighteen, we're done.

"You wanna go to the park, honey? Go on the swings?"

I glare at her. "Maybe ten years ago."

Then this picture comes in my mind. A picture of Sheila. Our first date. I took her to the park. She liked the swings. I pushed her once and she kept going. I stood on the swing next to her and watched her go high, high like the birds. She was a bird to me, she flew in my body. I could feel her wings flutter inside me.

Now when I look at her, there's just coldness. There is no bird anymore. I would give anything to touch her again.

"Have you spoken to your father?"

I look up. Mother's still here. Did I think she disappeared? The Dad question is good. Dad did phone. Last week. First time in months. His voice was scratchy. Bad connection from Sri Lanka. Said he might come for a visit next Xmas. I wonder what he looks like now. I told him I wished he was here but the line kept breaking up. I kept having to repeat everything I said and he still couldn't understand me.

"No," I tell this woman who is my mother. "I keep missing him when he calls."

"Too bad." She gulps her coffee. She's very far away. I know she's on the chair across from me, the TV behind her, the picture of the scarecrow on the wall hanging over. But she's at least a block away. And the chair she's sitting on is rolling away. Smooth and steady, like in the movies, she's getting smaller and smaller until I can't see her anymore.

Grandma touches my arm.

SKUD

"Have another doughnut, darling." Her voice is all sweet and powdered sugar just like her doughnuts. I smile at her and take one. It tastes so good.

Practice goes exceptionally well today. The ice is wonky and a couple of my shots lift on the bumps and hit Number Eleven in the head. I have nothing against Number Eleven, apart from the fact that he skates on his ankles and doesn't know how to hold the stick. Eleven's only practical use is being a deflector. The first puck that hits him bounces off his head and sets up a perfect pass. Smooth-skating Jake picks it up and shoves it past the goalie. I don't know why the puck lifts up the second time, but through some fluke, it hits Eleven on the head again, bounces in front of Jake who shoots but unfortunately hits the goalpost. Jake blames Eleven's head, saying it put a bad spin on the puck. I suppose it's possible, though you can't blame Eleven's head for everything.

When we head to the showers, Coach motions me over.

"Come to my office," says the Fat Man.

This is an interesting turn of events. Am I in trouble for the head work on Eleven? His office is a little hole near the shower room. A tower of old issues of *Hockey News* are piled on the corner. There's a curled-up picture of him and Wayne Gretzky smiling at the Hockey Hall of Fame. He never skated with Wayne or anything. He just happened to be there the same day as the Great One and slagged in for a photo-op.

The bags under Coach's eyes are big today, like little perogies. He has that look on his face. I'm thinking, Who died?

Turns out it's me.

"I'm putting you on the fourth line, Brad."

I've been first line since my first year. This is like being sent to Siberia.

"What's my sin, Coach?"

"No sin. You're my man. It's just, the game has changed."

These are not words I want to hear. My skin is bristling, my face is flushing but I just look at him very calm.

"What does this mean, the game has changed?"

"The referees are calling all the physical contact now. If we're gonna win games, the team has to flow. That means pure, natural skaters."

"I'm a great skater."

"You got guts but not the speed. Or the stick-handling. You'll be great on the fourth line, doing the damage you always do."

"Not if I don't get any ice time."

"You'll get some. Not like the old days, but you'll still play plenty."

I stare at the chunky porker, wanting to take his Gretzky photo and jam it in his eye socket.

SKUD

"Whatever's best for the team," I say, wondering how his NHL letter opener would look buried between his ribs. He smiles.

"I'm glad you're taking it so well, Brad. You've got a great attitude. You're a real team man."

"You know it, Coach. So who's my replacement?"

Coach smiles, about to unveil his masterstroke, the idea that will make his place in history.

"Charlie Norris. A great find."

This name is unfamiliar. He's from another league, I figure. And not from around here. Anybody this good is a name I would know.

"Who is this Charlie Norris?"

"You know her. Charlene."

"You're kidding me, right?" I say.

"No, Brad, I'm serious. She's the top player in the girls' league, but it's in bad shape right now. Her coach thought she could profit from playing with us this season. And us too."

I'm reeling. "Okay, "I say, "but why put her on the first line?"

"Have you seen her on the ice? She skates like Bure, stickhandles like Sakic. She gives us speed up the middle."

So now I know. I'm dumped for a skrunk. He's skrunking me.

"She can't check," I tell him. "She can't spear. She can't put anyone into the boards."

"We all have to change. That aspect of the game isn't being emphasized anymore. Finesse is now the word."

"I understand," I say and start to go.

"You're a real leader, Brad," he says. "I truly admire your maturity and commitment."

I walk out. I do not kick the door, I do not put my fist through the wall, I do not smash his red nose into sludge. He, better than anybody, knows from where I came. Since I was seven years old, he and his buds and my dad trained me to smash and reap the reward. For them I gave my flesh, my bone, my teeth. For them I take the pills. For the last ten years I've been their sluggo man, the one they love. And today I'm slagged. For a skrunk.

 Surveillance is all about seeing. Put your eye on the target, and you see it for what it really is. Take your eye off, and you're blind. The target's in your imagination and imagination is confusing, makes your brain go soft. If you stop seeing reality, you lose what's real. Then the enemy can manipulate you, destroy you. Imagination is killing the world.

After school I wait for Sheila. I know the door she exits from, the one closest to the drama studio. I watch across the street by a tree that provides good cover from that angle. I need to watch her. I need to know. Is it just Scoob who takes up the space where I was? How many does she have to fill the gap?

"Hey, Tom!" I turn to the voice, coming up from behind me. A straggler. My cover leaves me wide open to that side. I want to kick myself but it couldn't be helped.

I put on my charming face. "How're you doing, Jake?" I give an easy smile to this guy, the captain of the soccer team. I know what it's about. "Jake, I'm sorry, but there's no point asking. I can't do the team this year."

"Listen, the coach spoke to the Commander. It took some negotiating but I think they've worked out a deal so you can do both."

"I thought it was a dead thing."

He punches me in the shoulder. "You think I'm going to lose my best striker because of schedule conflict?"

"Okay," I smile. "I'm in."

He sighs this big relief. "That's great, man, great. We need you."

Just then, three grade nines run up to us. Jake gives me a wink. "Here come your groupies."

"Hey, Bertie." I'm always polite to this kid with braces, a grade niner who's just joined the Cadets. He's with three other kids his age who look at me like I'm some kind of rock star.

"This is him, this is him!"

"Nice to meet you." It's a little guy with ears that stick out. "Is it true? Are you really gonna fly F-16s?"

"That's the plan. If I get accepted into flight school."

"If? The Commander says you're the best cadet he's had in the last ten years. "

I shrug. "He's just being nice. It's pretty competitive." I glance at Sheila's door. No movement yet.

"Don't believe him!" Bertie tells his pals. "Commander said with his record Tom can do whatever he wants." His eyes are shining.

"I hope he's right." Truth is, the Commander did say it. Told me I'm a shoo-in for flight training. But I'm supposed to demonstrate a proper attitude to the new ones. Humility. Respect. Good manners.

The kids go and Jake turns to me. "I'm meeting everybody for subs, Tommy. You want to come?"

"Thanks for asking, Jake, but I'm waiting for a friend."

"Somebody new? I thought you might give Sheila another chance."

He thinks I broke up with her, not the other way around. Me dump her. "I'm thinking about it."

He makes this sheepish smile. "Whatever you do, man, leave something for the rest of us, okay?"

He gives me a punch and strolls away. The skin on my neck is clammy with cold and sweat. How can they not see me? How can they not know what's in my head?

I keep waiting. The school's dead now, no more surprise stragglers, no more interruptions forcing me to act like someone they think I am. At the end of one hour, I see her. Sheila. She comes out with some girlfriends, doing the chat and laugh. I can't hear what they're saying. I wait to see if Scoob comes too, but no. I hang back and let them turn the corner. Then I shadow. Sheila and her two girlfriends enter Barry's Bagels. This is the place Sheila and me used to sit for hours together. Doing homework, talking to friends. We'd hold court, the king and queen. But now I am dethroned.

I stay across the street, good vantage point. Sheila gets a foamy coffee, the same kind I used to buy her. Her friends buy diet colas. The one with the big earrings leaves first. Then the other one goes to the washroom.

She's by herself. I maintain position, the Commander's instructions on proper surveillance ringing in my ears: "Hold your position. Never reveal yourself to the subject."

But then I feel it. A magnetic pulse beaming out of Barry's Bagel's. It locks on me, starts pulling me. I grab the tree to stop the force from drawing me in, but the pull is too strong. My fingers lose their grip, my feet slide on the sidewalk, I'm being dragged to her. She's the sun, she has all the gravity in the solar system. Her force is too powerful. I cannot resist.

Through the doors I blow, the smell of corned beef smacking me like a wet wall. Suddenly I see myself standing over her. And her sweet perfume wafts over me, burning through the stinking food clouds, burning through me. I stand over her. She looks up, eyes so green, cat eyes stare at me.

"Hi, Tommy." Her coffee-tinged voice so smooth, so soft. Her voice pierces me like a porcelain bullet.

"Friday night. I'll take you to dinner. A movie."

She smiles. "No, thanks."

"Saturday night, then. To Cardinelli's. Like we used to."

She shakes her head. "I'm busy, very busy."

"When then? I want to see you."

"What you did in the Cage was stupid. Barbarian shit. It's one thing to fight for a reason. But not that crap."

"That's not me. I'm not like that."

She sips on her foam. "Then why were you in the Cage beating up Andy?"

"I love you. I got upset."

"You don't love me, Tommy. Love isn't about pounding a guy's head in."

"You're right, I was being stupid. I just lost it. I'm really sorry."

"I'm not the one you should be apologizing to."

"You're right. I'll tell him. I was wrong."

"It's good that you can say that."

"I'm changing. I'm trying. For you."

"Tommy, listen, we're better off just being friends."

"Friends, okay. Friends get together, right? How about this weekend?"

"I told you I'm busy."

I had her once, I blinked and lost her. Didn't know what I had. The second she says it's over, the

95

SKUD

arrow goes through me and I know I cannot live without her.

"Excuse me." The waiter tries to nudge past, touching me. Nerves start ringing. Fingers make a fist. I want to punch him hard in the throat, crush his bulging Adam's apple. Then I see Sheila, watching. Unravel fingers. Let him go.

"So when? Whatever is good for you, Sheila. I'd just like to, you know, keep trying. Work on the communication. Like you wanted."

She sighs. Shakes her head. Every movement of her head moves the air, making turbulence. I can see the shock waves moving toward me, smacking my head and, like a bell, the throbbing starts again.

I want to lift up the table, throw it across the room. Take that asshole waiter and toss him out the window, through the glass, his blood splattered on every little piece.

"Hi, Tommy, how're you doing?" It's Sheila's friend. She's smiling at me. She likes me. "You're not in uniform today."

"It's not a dress day," I smile, my mask on tight.

"Too bad. You look really good in that uniform."

"You don't have to say that." I glance at Sheila but she's not looking. She doesn't care.

"But it's true. You do." She gives me a little tickle with her finger, moves past me and sits down next to Sheila.

Sheila turns to her. "Let's run those lines."

I look at her, my eyes hollow. "It was good to see

you, Sheila. If you figure out a night, any time, just call, okay?"

She nods yes but means no. I look sadly at her nice friend. She shrugs consolation. But that's not what I need.

All my life, the love just dies around me. Some people, they just swim in it, they get born loved and it never ends. I don't know why some get it and some don't. I don't know why I am one who is shut out in the darkness.

She loves me, she loves me not. She loves me, she loves me not. Not. Not. Not.

 My mom goes completely wireless when she sees my face, so I tell her I ran to catch the bus, tripped and fell flat on my face. If I had fallen a millimeter to the left, a stick would've taken my eye out, so I was really very lucky.

"Who beat you up?" is her instant response, which doesn't do a lot for my confidence as an actor.

"Some Neanderthals," I reply, refusing to name names.

"I'm calling the police."

"Don't," I tell her. "I've got things under control."

"What does that mean?" she asks. And I decide to let her into the loop a little.

SKUD

"I've found a protector," I explain. "Things are going to be fine now."

She gives me one of her long, probing looks. I stare back without blinking, signaling to her that I'm not messing with her. So she gets down to business, insisting that I put anti-bacterial cream on every scratch. Which I guess is a good thing, because if I got flesh-eating bacteria in any of those wounds, they'd have to cut off my head to stop the infection.

I am feeling like they might as well amputate my head. Biggest break of my life and the coach of my dreams won't coach me. I spot Shane by the doors after school and am dying to ask again.

"Hey, Shane," I say, hoping he will somehow read my mind.

But his mind is elsewhere. "I gotta blow," he says and takes off.

I decide my only choice is to follow him and try to glean a lesson from observation. You may not have heard of the great Russian director Stanislavsky because he died a million years ago, but he's the big god of acting training. Ben Affleck, Johnny Depp and me, we all pray to him. He taught actors to be observers, so this is what all the great actors do, observe.

I walk about a half block behind him so that Shane doesn't spot me. He crosses the street and goes into Barry's Bagels. I wait to see if he's staying or going. He's in the line-up ordering take-out.

Then I notice somebody else watching the café. My nemesis, Tommy, is huddled behind a tree, staring inside. I wonder if he's tailing Shane too, but then I see through the glass that Sheila's in there with two of her pals. I'm just relieved that Dr. Jekyll/Mr. Hyde isn't tailing me.

Shane comes out holding a take-out bag and starts walking. I follow, making sure I'm out of sight. Then he stands at a bus stop and waits. Now I'm in a quandary. If he gets on a bus, how do I get on without him seeing me? The answer to my question comes in a pair. Some higher power definitely wants me to follow him, because not one, but two buses pull up. This is absolutely an act of God, because in Vancouver, you're lucky to see two buses in a day at the same stop. Shane gets in the first bus and I crawl into the second.

I sit near the front so I can keep an eye on who gets on and who gets off in the first bus. I'm thinking there is no down side to this journey. I'm researching my character, and since Shane is my character, everything he does is useful. Let's say he's about to do a big drug deal. As long as I stay at a safe distance, I should be able to get a good look at how a drop is made, the money exchanged, even what these guys do with their hands.

Hands are a big deal when you're acting. The minute you're on the stage, your hands become huge. Do you just stand there with them at your sides? Twiddle your fingers? Put them in your pockets?

SKUD

Bite your nails? Once you know what to do with your hands, you have your character nailed. So I spend a lot of time looking at Shane's hands.

But Shane could be also setting up a hit right now, and if I'm a witness, it could mean big trouble. The cops could try to use me to testify, and if I'm forced to, I would become a liability to Shane. I'd explain that I'd never talk, but he'd know I'd probably break after ten hours of violent interrogation, so he'd have no choice but to shoot me in the head. My plan is to stay far enough back that I can't be spotted. I feel a little weak kneed at the thought of watching somebody be murdered, but it is exactly the scene I have to play. The Qualm Brothers want real. Once I've seen an actual hit, I'll know exactly how to be real. I'll even know what to do with my hands.

The bus must stop two dozen times before I see Shane get off. As soon as my bus pulls over, I jump out. He turns around a corner and walks down a side street. I lean against the window of a discount eyeglass shop and watch him go. When I figure I'm out of his sight, I trail after him.

What's weird is that I can't figure out what kind of job he's onto this side of town. This is where Vancouver General Hospital is, and all around here are medical clinics and pharmacies and lots of people. An unlikely venue for a covert homicide. Then again, maybe it's perfect. Crowds, not a lot of cops. He passes a sandwich shop that's packed with nurses and doctors on their lunch break. For a second he pauses and I think this is it. Go in, blow the target away. People screaming, tables turning over, blood spurting everywhere and Shane quickly exits in the confusion.

But Shane doesn't go in to pop anybody off. He just keeps walking till he comes to the front entrance of the hospital. The doors swing open and he goes in. He walks to an elevator and steps in. I lurch over to it and watch where the numbers stop. Four. Thinking fast, I decide to take the stairs. As I'm pounding up them, I realize the truth. Shane's come here to make a score. The take-out bag isn't filled with bagels, it's filled with cash. Shane's got a deal going with a doctor who sells him prescription drugs. The doctor could have heavy gambling debts, or just be in it for the money. It's a great scam and the drugs are pure.

I get to the fourth floor and open the door a crack. The hallway looks clear. There's nobody here at all. Except for Shane. He's looking in at an empty operating room. He's staring through the glass at the oxygen tanks and scanners and the table where they cut people open. Is this where he's meeting for the drop? But nobody shows up. He just keeps peering in at the empty operating room. Then, after what must be like ten minutes, he heads right toward me.

He doesn't look happy. In fact, he has this haunted look on his face. Like he's seen a ghost.

This is not good. His connection didn't appear so he must be ready to slice. If he finds me spying on

101

him, he won't be overjoyed. So I tear down the stairs. I get one floor below him when the door opens and I hear him start coming down. Now I take very quiet steps, just trying to stay ahead of him. But he's gigantic and is doing two steps at a time. I move faster, hoping he'll just think I'm a nurse or a visitor or some normal human being using the stairs. Then I hear his footsteps stop. A door open. He's out on the second floor.

I charge back up the stairs and peek through the door. I don't see him so I step into a corridor. The sign says Spinal Injury Unit. The doctor he's scoring from must be in this ward. Makes sense. Back injuries require major boosts of painkillers. The nurse at the station is busy on the phone so I glide past her. And I start peeking into all the rooms, trying to spot Shane.

I'm getting nowhere fast. All I'm seeing are people in traction or with their heads all wrapped up like mummies. He's probably huddled in some locked office making the deal, and I'm out here wandering the hallway.

I figure I might as well make my exit. I've lost him and if I'm not careful, I could bump into him and that wouldn't look good.

Just as I turn to go, I hear a familiar voice. It's a woman's. An old woman's. At first I can't place it. Then I remember.

Miss Post, the English teacher. The one they say Shane threw down the stairs.

I like the coincidence. I imagine telling the Qualm Brothers this story when I audition. This banger I know broke a teacher's back. Now he scores major pharmaceuticals from her doctor. It's so evil it's elegant. They'll love it. Maybe they'll even want to buy the rights to the story. I heard the guy who wrote the Spiderman screenplay got a high six-figure deal for an idea. Seven hundred thousand plus, for nothing more than a thought. Makes you think.

Shane must be in some office down the hallway. I figure I may have missed the scene, but it was time well spent. Before I take off, I decide to peek in Miss Post's room, just to see how bad you look after Shane throws you down a flight of stairs. Her voice is like I always remember.

"I can wade Grief – whole pools of it – I'm used to that – but the least push of Joy breaks up my feet – And I tip – drunken…"

Yeah, I know nobody talks like that. But Miss Post never speaks like an actual human being. She is always quoting a poet, like right now it's Emily Dickinson, who she believes inhabits her body.

I peep in and there she is. She's got a serious neck brace on and her legs are in some kind of weird traction. The person she's talking to is bent down. I can't see who it is. There's no chance I'm going in. I only had her for one class and she gave me a C. Besides, she has company.

But then the person she's talking to sits back up and I see who it is.

SKUD

Shane.

I'm stunned. What's he doing here? It's too terrible to consider. First he pushes her down the stairs and now he's come back to finish her off. I can't imagine the kind of hatred he must feel for her. My heart's pounding as he reaches into his take-out bag, the one that should be filled with the drop-off cash. I almost charge into the room to stop him but I'm frozen, I'm too much a coward. What will he use – a gun or knife? A knife, I guess, or a garrote, something quiet.

I don't breathe as I watch his hand slowly emerge from the bag, gripping a…raisin bagel. He tears off a piece and feeds it to her.

"Delicious," she says and smiles at him. Shane smiles back.

I lurch from the door and flip down the stairwell. I can't get my head to stop whirling. What did I see?

First I thought it was someone else.

Not a good else.

The else that's been behind me all month. Letting me know he's watching. Waiting. Till he's ready.

But I'm ready too. I'm always ready. Now I'm readier than ever.

But this was not my shade. Not the cold hand.

This was Andy. Wanting some of me to rub off on

him. So I went where I go, let him follow and take what he thinks he needs.

I like his eyes. So clean. Never been used.

He's never seen anything.

BRAD At dinner I chew slowly and do not speak. Father Mine is chewing even slower than me. It's like the weight of all mankind rests on his shoulders.

"These string beans are from California," Mother Mine says, attempting to bring some levity and cheer to the table. "I hear that string beans are excellent for skin tone. Have some more, Bradley."

I take another serving and eat them one at a time. First I bite the top off, then the bottom. Then I split open the middle and eat the seeds and then the pod. I do this again and again.

Until Father Mine speaks.

"Don't you know how to eat a goddamn string bean? Quit picking at the things!"

Mother Mine turns pale. "Don't talk to him like that, Jerry."

Father Mine's color goes red. He jams his fork into his steak.

"Coach phoned me. Told me the news."

I am not surprised. This information is being kept quiet and I have told no one. But Coach and Father

SKUD

Mine are old pals. I bite another top off a string bean. Mother Mine stares at her plate.

"Coach says it's a new game now," I say.

"Coach clocked your skating," replies Father Mine. "Sixth slowest on the team."

"I thought speed wasn't everything."

"It is now," he says, digging his fork deeper into his T-bone.

"You're still on the team," says Mother Mine.

He glares at her. "Do you know who got his spot?"

She shakes her head.

"A faster skater. A better stickhandler. An all-around better player. On loan from the female league."

"But I thought you were the best player on the team, Bradley," says Mother Mine.

"I turned out to be expendable," I reply.

"That's the attitude that got you where you are. That's the kind of thinking that slows you down. Now look where it got you."

These are words that I want to turn into big crusty lumps and shove back down his throat. He taught me to skate, he taught me the attitude, he taught me the whole game. His words. I molded you, I turned you into a hockey machine.

And now, it's all wrong. I'm all wrong.

Father Mine eats another potato. I watch him chew and swallow, hoping he'll choke on it.

I break open the middle of another string bean.

Put the seeds on my plate and crush them into paste with a spoon. I'm thinking about other lessons Father Mine taught me. About enemies. That enemies are smashed into the boards. Ground into the ice. Annihilated.

I go outside and sit in my car. I turn on the ignition and floor it in reverse. The sound is loud enough to shake the windows. I imagine the front window breaking and a shard of glass flying into Father Mine's throat. I imagine myself holding him and crying, begging him to live, his blood pouring out on my hands.

I love him and I hate him. I would kill him and I would save him. Maybe that's the secret of his child-rearing technique. Love/Hate. It's hard keeping both ideas in your head at once.

I take the GT down Fraser Street. This time of night the street is dead so I go faster. The light at 16th starts to turn yellow. I push the gas and make it through on the red. The light goes crimson at King Edward. I ignore it, like I'm bursting through an invisible gate. Another red at 33rd I keep going. Nothing can stop me. I'm soaring, I'm pushing past a hundred and I whip past the stores like a bullet.

Then I see it in the rearview. The flashing lights. The men in blue.

For a second I think I should stop. Then I reconsider. My car's faster than theirs, and they're three blocks behind. I push it up to a hundred ten, hundred twenty, flip through the light at 41st. They're

SKUD

gaining on me. And another squad car joins the chase. If I don't do something quick they'll outmaneuver me. So I push the pedal harder, then at 48th I jerk the steering wheel left, burning rubber on the corner, then another fast right, fly down a side street, tear up a back lane, flip into somebody's carport, turn off the engine and lie down on the seat.

My heart is pumping. It's good to be alive.

I hear the sirens whining in the distance and I look through the sunroof at the moon. It's like a shining hockey puck in the sky. And in the moon, I see a face. Charlene, Hockey Queen. At first I want to scream. Even the moon's pulling my chain. All I want is to erase that face, blot it out of the sky, out of my life, out of the rink. I'd like to melt the ice she skates on, drown her in it. Drown them all.

And it hits me. Why not? Why not go for a meltdown? I'm no fall guy, I'm nobody's stooge. But they would make me that. They would rub my face in it.

I will not go down alone. Because I know everything is achievable if you set your mind to it. For example, I heard from somebody that Charlene's daddy owns a hardware store.

Suddenly I need some supplies.

TOMMY Thursday nights are best. It's the only night the pounding in my head stops. The only time Sheila's eyes are not shoved against my mind.

Thursday night is Cadet night. I sit in my room, polish my boots until they turn into black mirrors. In my uniform, I can feel the angel inside me. My buttons shine. There's not a crease on me. Grandma inspects me at the door.

"You look like your grandfather before he went off to fight those Nazis."

"Now that was a war."

Her eyes water up. "So many died."

"But they got Hitler. They nuked the Japanese."

She mutters and shakes her head. "Such a price."

They had some great planes then. B-17 Flying Fortress, the B-29 Superfortress. They carpet-bombed Germany. And the fighters. I wish I had a chance to fly a P-51 Mustang. Now that was a great fighter. It could only go 487 miles per hour but in those days it was the best. Three machine guns on each wing, 2000-pound bombs. The most fearsome thing in the air.

At the armory I run the drills, then the Commander does the inspection. I love to stand and have him look me up and down, checking every button, every fold, every hair. Then he smiles at me. "Good, Sergeant, at ease," and I know I did everything right, that I am right. In the right place, in the right way, in the right time. For you this is nothing,

SKUD

maybe. Maybe you always feel right. But me, never. Except with the Commander. He has a soldier's eyes, neutral eyes. They just observe and when he says, "At ease, Sergeant," I know I can relax. I let the air out of my lungs and my shoulders come down and there's peace inside because I know everything about me is right. Once a week, I'm right.

Then the Commander brings up a sore topic. "I presume most of you are aware of past casualties to our forces in conflicts overseas."

Everyone nods. Some of our ground troops were killed and wounded by allied fire. It was all over the headlines.

"We call it fratricide: the use of friendly weapons with the intent to kill the enemy or destroy his equipment that results in unforeseen and unintentional death or injury to friendly personnel. In the Gulf War, twenty-five percent of all allied casualties were fratricidal in nature. Who can tell me why this happens?"

Bertie steps forward. "Technology, sir. Sophisticated weapons can malfunction. Their speed and range reduce reaction time so you can't tell friend from foe."

I speak up. "Environment, sir. Darkness, weather and terrain complicate identification."

"Both are true. But the number one cause is human. Stress of combat, inadequate training, lack of experience and simply not being on the ball." He takes a hard, long look at everyone. "One out of four in the Gulf War. Look at the people around you. Imagine one quarter of you dead. Killed by friendly fire. By your allies or by each other. Does that sound like a positive?"

"No, sir!" fifty of us say together.

"There'll be improvements in technology. Electronic IDs, smart weapons. But the real issue for every one of you is situational awareness, discipline under fire and just plain using your brains. Now where are your brains – on your shoulders, or up your asses?"

"On our shoulders. Sir!"

"Point to them!"

Fifty fingers point at their heads.

"When the time comes, when you're in the line of fire, remember that! Keep your head on your shoulders, not up your butt!"

"Yes, sir!"

After the drills, I come out of the armory, walk past the two Cruiser Tank Mk I's guarding the entrance, their 75-mm cannons filled up with cement.

"Hey, Tom."

I look up and see Brad sitting on top of one of the tanks.

"How come I can't get inside this thing?"

"Because it's just for show."

He laughs. "Like everything else around here."

"Not true and you know that."

"But you never get to use it."

SKUD

"I will. Soon enough. What's your problem?"

"Nothing, I was just thinking about you. About your position. What if the Commander flipped on you?"

"How do you mean?"

"As in, said one thing and did another. Like pulled off your wings."

"Why would he do that?"

"Because people are ephemeral. They change their minds. They say one thing and do another. They lie. They cheat. They betray."

"He won't. I'll be in the air. In an F-16."

Brad shakes his head. "Things change."

"Maybe for some people. Not for me. I've been working hard a long time for this. Everybody wants this for me too."

I think of myself a mile in the sky, looking down at buildings as small as pinpricks. Of breaking the sound barrier. Of never coming down.

Brad spits on the ground, then smiles at me.

"Yeah, they do, don't they? You're their perfect guy."

"I wouldn't go that far."

This hard little laugh, almost like a bark, comes out of him. "No, you are, Tom. You're the top gun, the main guy. That's you." Brad jumps off the tank and into his car.

I watch him drive off. Something is bent in Brad. For the last week he's barely talked to me. He looks worse than he does after a bad game.

I put my hand up to the cannon, tap my fingers on the cement plugging up the muzzle. They built hundreds of these tanks in World War II, but they never saw any action. Just used for training. And now they're filled with cement.

At home, Grandma's sipping on her late-night beer. It helps her sleep. She looks up at me.

"Is something troubling you, Thomas?"

"No, Grandma."

She smiles. "You look so much like your father. It's like he's here in this room." I just shrug.

"I'm sorry you had such a bad visit with your mother."

"It wasn't that bad."

"I could tell you were upset."

I wasn't upset. I wanted to rip her throat out. But I clamped myself down.

I look at my grandma, so kind, so nice. The one who saved me from my mother.

"I'm just sorry for what she puts you through, always trying to get your money," I say.

"It's never too bad, Thomas."

"But it is. I hate it when she hurts you."

"I'm not hurt, darling. Have a little snack."

I shake my head and go upstairs.

SKUD

ANDY

Video stores are excellent research. I like to go in and study the covers. What I'm doing is checking the attitude and poses. Wesley Snipes is always worth emulation. This is a guy who invented himself as an action hero. He's totally buff, sure, but not a true martial-arts hero like Van Damme or Jet Li. He just has the look and you buy it. I pull all the movies of his I can find and check his face. He doesn't show much but you feel the rage simmering underneath. It's like, don't push my button if you want to live.

I try to find some of that, try to match the tone. I check my face with a hand mirror.

Nothing. Just pudgy cheeks. So I try to layer in some subtext. I think about Brad and Tommy. I remember the belt, the kicks, the strip. Now I look in the mirror again. I'm transformed. I've got the Wesley Snipes sneer. I look like a guy who could waste a terrorist army single-handed. I look like the Man.

I do a close-up to check the eyes. I narrow them for the burning-death look. Very Wesley. Then I feel someone behind me. Another eye appears in the mirror. It's Shane's.

"What're you looking at?"

"Something in my eye."

"I saw you ogling yourself."

"Okay, I'm busted. I'm trying to copy the look."

"You're getting it off video covers?"

"I'm a desperate man."

Shane shakes his head. I can't tell from his lips whether he's frowning or smiling.

"Pathetic," he finally mumbles.

"Why not? I heard Mafia guys get all their moves from the Godfather movies."

"Wasn't there a Mafia before the Godfather movies?"

"Yeah, but they weren't as cool till the movie showed them how to do it."

He stares at me with those heavy lidded eyes. Sighs. Then he says, "C'mon, I'll teach you a few things."

"Are you serious? That's too good!"

I grin so big my face feels like cracking. My dream come true. Shane taps me on the chin.

"First thing you got to learn. Don't let it show on your face."

We walk a couple of blocks over to a park. I'm so pumped I can barely stand it. I've got an authentic banger on side! He wasn't just in a gang, he ran one! That's what the Qualm Brothers want. Real. And now I've got real. I score!

Shane stands on the pitcher's mound and nods for me to come over. "What do you want to learn first?"

"The moves," I say.

"There aren't any moves. It's just knowing what to do."

"Okay, okay, so show me what to do."

"About what?"

SKUD

I'm thinking fast, because I'm afraid he'll take off without showing me anything, but first I have to think of something for him to show me.

"Okay, let's say somebody pulls a gun on you. What's the correct response?"

"Does he say what he wants?"

"Let's say he wants your money."

Shane nods, thinking. Then he takes my hand, closes it. Then lifts my thumb and pulls out my index finger.

"There's your gun. Stick me up."

This, I'm telling you, feels very weird. I'm pretending my finger's a gun and pointing it at a true killing machine.

"Gimme your money," I say, trying to sound like I mean it. He just stands there, his eyes not looking at me. I'm bracing myself, waiting for the fast move that'll twist my wrist back. Will he break it?

"Gimme your money!" I repeat.

Then, very slowly, he reaches behind him.

"What're you doing?" I ask, and I move my finger against his belly. "Be cool, be cool," says Shane. "I'm just getting my wallet."

And he holds out his wallet and hands it to me. "Take what you want." And he puts his hands at his sides.

I'm still waiting for the big move, but it doesn't happen.

"Is that it?"

He nods. "Yeah. That's what you do."

"Where's the quick moves, the Jackie Chan?"

"In real life, Jackie Chan's dead every time. You can't beat a gun. If you can't beat something, you surrender. Unless you don't want to live."

"Okay, okay, but that's guns. Maybe they're just too high stakes. What if somebody pulls a knife on you?"

Shane bends down and picks up a stick.

"You mean, like we're in a fight, and I pull out a knife?"

"Yeah." This is more like it.

"What would you do?"

I take off my jacket and wrap it around my arm.

"Okay, I'm ready."

He raises an eyebrow. "What's that for?"

"To stop the blade without it cutting me. I can't remember what movie I saw it in."

He nods, looking impressed. "Haven't seen that one before. Looks interesting."

And before I see it, he sticks the twig in my stomach.

"Hey, I wasn't ready," I protest.

"You're never ready for a knife," he says, and I can see some kind of sadness in his eyes.

"Give me a chance." I hold out my wrapped arm for defense. A snake striking, he jabs me in the neck. I reach up but he jabs me in the ribs, on my thigh, in the shoulder. I turn, and I feel the branch break against my back.

"Stop, stop! I'm dead, okay!"

"No, you're not. You need a couple hours to die."

I'm like completely humbled. He's quicker than anything I've ever seen.

"Nobody's that fast."

"You're right," Shane agrees. "After the knife sinks in, taking it out slows things down. Especially if you get it caught in bone."

My stomach quivers in awe. He's a walking encyclopedia of death.

"So the wrapped jacket thing doesn't work," I admit. "Tell me what to do when attacked with a knife."

He doesn't miss a beat. "Run."

"That's it?"

"Maybe if you're lucky, you can outrun him. It's hard to stab somebody on the run."

"What if he throws it at you?"

He shrugs. "Odds are he's not holding a throwing knife."

"Somehow I don't feel like I'm learning the moves."

Shane smiles that sad smile of his. "Yeah, you are. These are them."

Suddenly he's real still. Looking, listening.

"What is it?"

"Sh."

I listen too but I don't hear anything other than the traffic in the distance. Some seagulls are fighting over an apple core. Kids playing somewhere. A lawnmower.

Then his big arm grabs me and throws me down on the ground. He's lying next to me. Watching. Listening.

I hear wheels screech to a stop. I peek out and in the distance, three guys get out of a shiny black van and peer out toward us. My stomach turns over as I see one of them pull out a gun and aim it in our direction. I start to sweat. His friends start laughing. He pretends to shoot it, the recoil throwing him back. His pals laugh harder. He puts the gun away, waves goodbye to us, and they screech off in the van.

Shane stands up.

"Who the hell was that?" I ask, shaking.

"Some old friends."

"It was your old gang, wasn't it?" His eyes look down for a second so I know it's true. "Were they just playing around or what?"

"Or what."

"How did you know we were being followed? I mean, I had no idea they were around."

"I knew," is all he says. Now my stomach relaxes a little.

"So you usually can tell if somebody's after you?" I ask.

"Especially when I buy bagels."

"You saw me!"

He shrugs. "You got lots to learn."

I know I should bite my tongue, but I can't help it. "Why were you visiting Miss Post?"

SKUD

"She's my friend," he replies. And I can see that his eyes look misty, which throws me.

"That's not what I heard."

"What you heard is the skud," he mutters. "She's a great person. She gave me words."

This is weird. I wouldn't have guessed that one. He catches the look on my face. And for a second I think I'm going to be butchered by him. Then he closes his eyes and breathes.

"I know what's going around. People think I pushed her."

"But you didn't."

"In a way, I did. The crew knew I liked her. Getting her was a way of touching me."

"Because you left the TMR?"

He just looks off in the distance. I realize that I should stop pursuing this direction.

"So what were you doing up in the operating rooms?"

He goes completely silent.

"I thought you were scoring or something," I say. He still doesn't respond so I keep talking. "But you were just staring through the glass, looking inside."

"Was I?"

I see he's got exactly the same, upset look on his face as when I saw him up there.

"Shane?"

He doesn't say anything.

He just walks away. And then he's gone.

SHANE

Those days I slept three, four hours a night. The rest I'd catch in class. One day, Miss Post woke me up. Dropped a book in front of me. What's this, I asked. This is a seed, she said. I'm planting it in you. Read it.

I carried it in my pocket for a week. Then I started reading pieces of it, whenever. Waiting for a score or a hit, I'd read. My brother laughs at me, doing homework. This isn't homework, I tell him. It's just some poems.

After class I'd turn off the cell and pager. Go find her and we'd talk about what I read.

One day she looked at me and said, some plants will crack through concrete, just to get to the sun. I think it may be cracking through you.

The crew looked for me. Found me talking with her. They couldn't understand it. You in love with that old bag? No, I said, I'm just…you know, home-work. And they'd laugh.

But later on, they figured out they were right. They could see what she put in me was cracking right through me.

So they cracked her.

SKUD

BRAD

It's a different world here on the rink. A week with our new teammate and the truth comes out. The Powers That Be, the bosses of the league, have dictated a new style on us. That's why Coach was sagging in front of me. Protecting his job was more important than protecting the team. Protecting me. And the rest of the team, shaking in their skates, bow down to the spineless fat man, and do what they're told.

And Father Mine? The lying bastard blames me for skating slow, for not improving my skills. Me, I'm just here biding my time, waiting for the right moment. Waiting for sweet revenge.

Meanwhile, practice is more figure skating than hockey. Everybody sliding like angels, trying to emulate the great "Charlie" Norris, queen of the rink, so happy to get the good strokes from that dickless blimp. Nobody's got the smooth moves like our new Number One. We're all mortals, sweating like pigs, trying to gain the finesse, the flow, flow, flow that comes so naturally to her. Even Number Eleven, head bandaged under his helmet, is trying to stick-handle like a Swede. I go to give him a little hip check and –

"BRAD! Watch the contact!"

Coach is like a referee on amphetamines. Every time I lift my stick or raise an elbow, he blows the whistle, following his orders from above.

But do I lose my smile? No. Do I let slip even a

twinge of discontent? Not on your life. I just smile and keep on with the play. Because I'm a team boy, an all-for-one, one-for-all kind of fellow. I know he's a man under the gun, under the thumb of powers so high and mighty he has no choice but to surrender everything he's ever believed in. Such a sacrifice he's made for the game. For his pension plan.

But then a little scent. A smell. Number Eleven, whipping behind the goal, stops and has a whiff. In a flash, everybody's stopped for a sniff.

Could this be smoke?

Yes. Great gray clouds pouring out. Eyes tearing, throats burning. Fire!

"FIRE!" screams Coach.

"FIRE!" screams Number Eleven.

"FIRE!" screams Charlie Norris, rink queen.

"Get low, get low!" the goalie yells. He took a Red Cross course, he knows where the oxygen lives. "Stay close to the ice, the good air's there!"

Now everybody's slip-crawling on the ice, worming it to the exit. And there's Coach, slapped on his big belly, pushing his beloved players away as he panics out the gate. Number Eleven is gasping, fighting to get out, but Coach is pulling at him, trying to break out first. My God, did you see that? Coach elbowed him. And now Coach executes a perfect hip check on poor Number Eleven who's flopping on the floor and Coach, like some hyperactive toddler, bullets on all fours through the outside door into the open air.

SKUD

An opportune moment to play the hero! I fight through the smoke and grab the wheezing Number Eleven.

"Relax, pal," I tell him. "You're in good hands." He looks up at me with grateful, ash-crusted eyes. He says something, but it just comes out as a whistle. Crawl-pulling, I drag him to the doors, smoke stinging eyes. Finally the light. Air.

So much can happen in fifteen minutes.

Now we're all outside, shaking in our skates, watching the firefighters hose down the building. Specifically, the locker room.

This is bad. This could do the season. Number Eleven is on oxygen, the medics hovering over him. Between smoke inhalation, his asthma and the shot he took from Coach in the ribs, he's had better days. I get many pats on the back for saving the poor boy's life.

Over there, you can see that Coach is speaking with the league boss. Coach is crying for his melted rink, for his ruined season. Seems the boss isn't delighted with Coach's less-than-courageous behavior at the exit. Number Eleven's daddy has just chewed his ear off. It seems he's a liability lawyer and has already mentioned, loud enough for all to hear, the million-dollar lawsuit he will be launching. And soon after that he's pumping my hand, thanking me for saving his only son's life. Thanks I accept with sincere humility.

And look over there, where the red lights are

beaming — yes, at the police cars. Notice a nervous someone being interviewed by our boys in blue.

Who might this anxious fellow be? Oh, my gosh. It's no fellow. It's Ms. Flow herself. Only this time, the flow isn't about her skate stride, it's the flow of tears.

But why is she crying as she speaks to our sturdy law enforcers? Oh, what a shock! It seems our heroine's locker was filled with flammables.

Very soon, disturbing information will rise to the surface. Did you know her daddy owns a hardware store? Did you realize the ignitable items were from that very establishment? Here, at the peak of her career, her locker exploded and took down the whole dressing room, the whole rink, the whole season, perhaps. Common wisdom is Charlie buckled under the pressure. Inside that free-flowing royal skin was an arsonist just burning to be free.

Alas, now all is charred and cindered. Nothing is left. Hockey is dead.

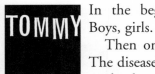 In the beginning, we're the same. Boys, girls.

Then one day the Serpent comes. The disease sets in. This bite from the apple that tears your mind up. And then they start to glow. They change color.

That's when I felt the Serpent, the worm inside

SKUD

my brain. It never stopped wriggling and growing. To be something I had to get something. Always, always, that whisper stabbing. Flesh. Desire.

All those daggers stabbing inside me, they all melted away the first time I saw Sheila. She has eyes that have the magic. Eyes that touch you and you turn better inside than you are into a giant, into an emperor. My insides finally matching what people saw on the outside. With her, I was pure. Her hand in mine, electric, was all I needed, all I wanted. Never anything else. That would drag her into the mud, soil her perfection. She's above all that dirty nothingness. Those pigs can want her and lust her but she's in another dimension, untouchable. Her feet never touch the ground.

No one can stop me from worshipping her. No one has to know. And one day, when she's ready, she'll smile on me again.

I sit in my room. I can feel the walls squeezing on me. I keep staring till they go wavy, like eels in the aquarium. I stare till I penetrate the camouflage and can see all the eyes in the walls. They see me, I see them.

I pick up phone and dial her number.

"Hello?"

Her voice. I can taste cinnamon.

"Hello? Who is this?"

I want to speak, I want to put on my good voice, my voice that everyone likes and respects. I want to tell her that with her I'm in equilibrium, my inside matches my outside, she makes me normal, she makes me whole. But nothing comes into my throat.

Click.

Why did she pretend not to know who it was? Was she with someone else? Scoob? Or another? Can she look away from them and back in my direction? She must have known it was me. Or maybe she didn't. Now I'm a ghost to her. She can't see me or hear me.

Maybe it's better that way. Here I am, in my hermit cave, my tiny cell, imagining her. Seeing her so perfect and beautiful and pure. I crouch here and let her sweetness wash over me. I don't need to touch her. No one can touch her.

I sit down to write her.

DEAR SHEILA.

I cross out the dear. What does dear mean? It falls a trillion light years short of saying the feeling in me. No weak, nothing words can go in front of her name.

SHEILA.

Her name so perfect. And then I put the only words that mean anything.

I LOVE YOU SO MUCH.

It needs more.

YOU YOU YOU.

And more.

I LOVE LOVE LOVE.

I look at it. So stupid. Skud nothing words. Letters shoved together, letters that mean nothing

SKUD

sitting alone, spread apart. Put them together and then there are words, words that mean even less. Words just lie there, they tell you nothing. Words are dud bullets. Words are lies. I love her, yes. But to write this down makes it limp, dead, wank. To love you show it, not write it down.

But how can I show it?

I take my combat knife. The Commander told us to always keep it honed. You can slice a hair with it. I run my thumb over the edge. The blade makes a little valley in the skin. Blood oozes up. I let it drip on the letter. One, two, three, four, five red drops splash over the words and the white paper.

I hold the cut closed. Five drops of love for her.

Sheila. I'll wait for you forever. Wait for me. I pray you.

 There was this king. Everything he touched turned to gold. I used to love that story when I was a kid. But I only knew the good part.

One day Miss Post gave me a book. Inside was the real way the story ended.

The king ran around touching everything. It was the happiest he ever was. Everything was so much better. He loved making everything sparkle. Then by mistake he touched the only person he loved.

She turned into gold.

He screamed. He cried. He begged the gods to take back the touch, to change her back. But it was too late.

Now everything was gold but he didn't want it anymore, he hated it, he hated his world of gold.

So finally he touched all his food. The cheese, the bread, the wine, the water. Turned it all to gold. And he sat down at the table and watched it sparkle. That's all he did. He watched the glitter. And starved to death.

 Father Mine was sad to hear of the demise of his beloved team. The whole episode has shaken him badly. Broken faces he can understand, but the destruction of a rink is incomprehensible. To make it worse, due to lack of available ice, our players were split up and sent to different teams. I was offered another position but I declined. It just wouldn't be the same playing with another team and a different coach, and the season's nearly over, I sadly told them. The truth is that nothing would feel better right now than crunching bones and pulping faces. I think about it all the time. But they won't let that happen. Those days are gone. And so am I.

Father Mine and I visited Coach, who is recovering from a minor heart attack at home. When he recovers, he'll be teaching remedial math. No more coaching for Coach. Poor fella.

SKUD

Amazing what one little match can do.

The Goddess Charlene's lucky streak continues. The police couldn't pin the arson on her. She was nowhere near the locker at the time and the good character testimonials poured in. Funny thing, though, everybody has doubts about her now. Did she crack up? Is she, under that fine athletic body, a raging psycho?

But now that she's been eliminated as a suspect, the police are stumped. Who could be the culprit?

The rink is across the street from the school, so they set up shop in the vice-principal's office and started pulling in members of the team for questioning. My meeting with Sergeant Luzio is short and sweet. In fact, Sergeant Luzio himself is short and sweet.

"That was brave of you, pulling out Norman like that."

I shrug it off. "Anybody would have done it."

"No, not anybody," he sighs. Then he eyes me. "I've seen you play, Brad, I like your game."

"Thanks, Sergeant. I do what I can."

"You're not afraid of contact. I admire that in a player."

Now I'm starting to wonder. Is this a set-up?

"Do you make it to many games?" I ask him.

"As many as I can. My son'll be on the team next year, if there is a team. I hear you were bumped down to the fourth line."

That's the question I'm waiting for.

"Yeah," I say, "I thought it was a good strategy. Let the pure skaters go up front and the crushers come in later. I just wish we could've seen how it played in action."

"Sounds like you're a real team man."

"Have been all my life."

He shakes my hand and wishes me all the best and I let the next suspect in for their interrogation.

Was I relieved? Satisfied? Let's just say, with the right fuse you can do practically anything. So is the revenge sweet? Yes. Am I satisfied? No. I'm a bottomless pit. I want to smash them all and keep smashing. I want to cover the whole world in their bloody pulp.

I stroll over to the rink to see the effect. The dressing room is a blackened shell. I step over the yellow police tape and go inside the rink. It's covered in soot and ash. I sit down in the stands and take it in, my stomach churning.

Once, this was me. No more. I'll never strap on the stinking blades again. They took it all from me, they stripped it and left me to rot.

I hear a voice. My chum. Tommy.

"Sorry to hear about the fire, Brad."

I nod. "It's a sad time for all hockey lovers."

"Guess the timing could've been worse."

I eye him. "In what sense do you mean?"

"I heard you were taken off the first line. Why didn't you tell me?"

"I was waiting for the proper moment."

SKUD

Tom runs his hand through his close-cropped hair. "I thought we were best friends."

"Forgive my silence," I say, a hot, vile taste rising in my throat. Mr. Wonderful, Mr. Air Force, comes here to my burnt-out palace to console me. But the condescension in his voice irritates like nails on chalkboard. He's still on top and knows it. I am on the bottom, humiliated, and he comes to me to cheer me up. Him, the king of the school. I feel like grinding his pretty face in the ashes and broken glass.

He gives me a sympathetic look. "Now what will you do?"

He is so swelled up with his good luck, with his bright future. They even made a special concession to get him on the soccer team.

Without even trying, I find myself pissing on his dreams.

"What choice do I have but weigh my options? Reevaluate my plans. Something you should do too."

Tommy takes the bait. "What do you mean?"

"Your flight plans."

His face tightens, his defenses going up. I can feel my mood lifting.

"I have a perfect plan and you know it. Next year, I'm starting F-16 flight school."

I shake my head in the most good-natured way.

"With all due respect, my compadre, you have neglected to consider the catheter."

"What're you talking about?"

"I just read it in an aeronautics mag. No toilets on those things. You leak into a tube, goes in plastic bag. Did you know this?"

Tommy gives a vague nod. "What about it?"

"This news report states this pilot, twenty thousand feet up, was changing his bag. It slipped. Piss spilled all over the computer. Sparks, short circuits. The plane went into a spin. He ejected. Coming down, the pee bag froze, banged him in the face, he went out cold, hit the ground, broke his neck. Killed by his own urine."

"That's complete B.S."

I sagely nod to my dearest friend, stoking the fire. "True story. Just like you. Mr. Premature Ejection."

Tommy's getting heated. I know this because he's taking regular, deep breaths. Here we are in this burnt-out rink, and he's sucking in oxygen so he doesn't flare up.

"Are you trying to say something to me?"

I'm very amused. I love flipping his off/on switch. "You're provoked."

"No, I'm not. Why would I be?"

I shake my head. "I think you're losing control."

"That is crap, Brad."

I study his face, taking a long time for the maximum unsettling effect. "We both know you have a control problem, even if the rest of the world doesn't know it."

"There is no problem."

I laugh. "We're friends, Thomas. I know that

133

SKUD

fighter pilots have to be in complete control of their emotions. I would never give away your secret."

"There's no secret."

"So you're saying nothing rattles you? You are a pure rock of control?"

"If I have to, I use guided breath and self-talk to deal with distracting emotions. That's how we are trained."

I love this. "You mean, breathing and talking to yourself?"

Tommy nods. "That's right."

"If you're so sure of yourself, how about we do a little test?"

"What do you have in mind?"

"You be a good officer. I'll say things to distract you from your mission. You control your emotions using the skills taught you in cadets."

He thinks about it. Nods. "Okay."

I should not do this. He is my best friend. If I proceed, I will make him bleed. Things will never be the same between us. But the sour taste in my mouth is getting worse. It's turning into acid and can't be stopped.

I look at my most recent handiwork, the charred smell wafting through my nostrils. And I look at him, the big man of the school, so straight and perfect, everything right for him, everything wrong for me.

The bile inside wins.

"Guess my agenda last night," I say, in the most matter-of-fact way I can manage.

"You went out?"

"Saw a friend. Of yours."

"Who?"

"Beautiful Sheila."

The cold chill that goes through him is so arctic I swear I can see frost on his nose.

"What?"

"I parachuted into her place. Her parents were absent."

"You're making this up."

I wag my finger at him. "You decide, Sergeant. She invited me. She wearing robe at door."

Tommy's getting flushed now. I never realized the pleasure inflicting torture can give a person.

"No," he says. "Her door is locked when she's home alone."

"When she saw me, she opened it. Just like that. First time for everything, she said." I see his temperature go up another couple of degrees. "Self-talk, soldier. Don't get provoked."

"First what?"

"First everything. First tour of the solar system. Mars, Mercury and Venus. I touched every planet."

I swear I see steam rising out of Tombo's collar. I remind him to keep breathing.

"I am breathing!" he snaps back.

"Good," I say. "I just want you to stay on top of it. Which, by the way, she said you never did. She said you never performed any of the things I performed on her. Said you tried once but failed."

SKUD

Tommy's trying not to buy it, but I know he is.

"She never said that."

"She's a biter, man. She screams."

"You're lying."

"Right on her parents' bed." I pull down my collar and show him a dark bruise. "Hey, note the hickey."

That does it for my self-controlled friend. He charges me, trying to get his hands around my neck. I take his wrists in each hand, pull them up and around, bend them back and presto! He's on the floor between the seats and I'm on top, pinning him down.

"Tommy, breathe. Be a hero. Don't let yourself get provoked."

His eyes are bloodshot, flaring. "If you touched her…"

"Think F-16. Think flying high over clouds, bursting the speed of sound, criss-crossing the globe."

"How could you?" he says, and I swear he's practically crying.

"Curiosity. Could I maintain over an hour? Answer: Yes."

"You touched her."

With all sincerity, I gaze in his eyes. "I'm not rude. I accept invitations."

He explodes. "I'll kill you!"

I let him go. It's wrong, twisting him like this. But it has an uplifting effect on my mood. Even better than smashing a nose into the boards. His pain is healing me, making me feel strong again. I look at him.

"Self-talk, breath exercises, where does it get you? Sorry, Tomster, you just failed the exam. Better luck next year, Sergeant."

Tommy looks at me, his eyes oozing clear liquid. "I thought you were my friend."

"I am," I smile. And he storms off.

He'll settle down soon. He gets wounded too easily. I admit I savored it, but is it my fault he puts himself above me? So what if I filled his head up with lies. He should know better than to be sucked in. If he can't withstand some bullshit about his ex-girlfriend, how is he going to fly a war plane? If anything, I did him, and our country's military, a favor.

It's amazing how much better I feel.

 So I get the call.

"Andy. It's Sally. The Qualm Brothers finished the rewrite. Your call-back is skedded for 4 P.M. Wednesday. Call to confirm."

I don't want to seem too anxious, so I wait five minutes before I phone her back.

Her voice is very, very friendly. "Hey, Andy! You gonna be there?

137

"I'm thinking about it," I joke, and she laughs, which is a good sign.

"Back at the Gastown Studios. You remember where it is?"

"Yeah, in Gastown."

Just before I hang up, she says one last thing.

"Preston had one bit of advice for the call-back, Andy."

"What was it?"

"Be real."

So now, of course, I have an ache in my gut. Be real. Somehow that's supposed to be helpful. Do people think that's easy, that being real, being genuine, is something you can just turn on or turn off?

Now I am in fear for my life. Wednesday! If I don't find Shane, I'm doomed. I need him to help me through this. He knows real. He is real. I can't be real without him.

My mom, of course, heard the message.

"Is this that piece of crap you auditioned for?"

"As far as I know."

She nods. "I'd wish you luck but you know I'd be lying."

"Thanks, Mom."

"You know why I'm letting you go without a fight?"

"Because you believe in personal freedom."

"Because I believe, in the end, that you're not a superficial asshole."

"Mother, you should wash your mouth out with soap."

"It was actually a compliment."

"Jeez, I missed that, thank you."

As I head for the door, she asks if my "protection" is still keeping me safe from the thugs that jumped me.

Yeah, I nod, he is.

Then she gives me her penetrating look. "Andy, this protector, why does he do it? Are you into something bad with him?"

I look her straight in the eye. "No, Mom, everything is very cool, believe me."

"Then what's in it for him?"

"I'm not sure." It's a good question. I can only guess at the answer. "He's kind of cut off from his... family. I guess he needs a friend."

"Well, you should invite him over sometime. I'd like to personally thank him for helping you out."

"Or do you mean check him out?"

"If you say he's cool, he's cool. I'm serious, he's welcome any time."

"For sure," I say and go, thinking that I'd love to except for the fact that I have no idea where he lives or how he lives, and I'm racking my brains trying to figure out where to find him.

Out of ideas, I go to the park hoping he'll show up there again. I'm sitting on the swings, watching some crows peck at a dead squirrel when I see a large shadow. He must have radar that's tuned right into my anxiety meter, because there he is.

139

"Am I glad to see you!" I bark. I'm not thinking about how it is he just happened to find me. I have a sneaking suspicion he follows me around and right now I'm glad for it. But then he steps out of the shadows and I get a good look at him. His eyes are all puffy and his clothes are a mess.

"What happened to you, man?"

"Nothing."

"You look like you haven't slept in a week." I know something has to be going on. "Is the TMR still hunting you?"

He simply changes the subject. "Did you hear anything about the part?"

I immediately perk up and tell him the good news. "I got a call-back. That means I'm on the short list!"

"Congratulations." I can tell he's genuinely happy for me because the right side of his mouth curls up a tiny bit. "So what do you need? I showed you moves."

"How about some back story?"

"What's back story?"

"To make a character real, you have to know his history. Where he came from, key events in his life, all the things that made him turn out the way he is."

Shane doesn't seem to quite know what I'm talking about.

"If you'll just tell me a little about that stuff with you, I can turn it into material I can use for my character."

He grabs the monkey bars with his hands and starts doing pull-ups.

"What do you want to know?"

"Like how you got how you are. Where'd you catch all this?"

Shane keeps going up and down. "Along the trail."

"Your whole life?"

"Sure."

I decide to ask him everything. "First fight?"

"Don't remember."

"Biggest fight."

"All big."

"Most important."

He climbs up on top of the bars and looks out, thinking. I go up too, but not too close. I don't want to look like I'm squeezing him. After about five minutes of silence, he finally says something.

"Grade six. Robert Flowers. A giant. He challenges. I win. Then all the big ones challenge. I beat them all. Or my brother does. Then we get offers."

"To beat people up?"

"Like a big cousin coming to revenge a black eye on his little cousin. We'd take him down for fifteen bucks. Or we'd just be standing at the playground at recess and a kid'd give us his lunch money to smash somebody."

I'm stunned.

"Like a bam in the face?"

Shane holds up his fist and pumps it in the air.

SKUD

"Like bambambambam. For three, four, five bucks, whatever they had. By the time we got to junior high, we were charging ten or twenty for the service."

"Why'd the price go up?"

"Everybody was bigger. And had bigger budgets."

"What did they do to deserve the service?"

Shane gives me a puzzled look. "I don't know, we just beat them up."

Then I get it. This was a thing he had to do. It was how he got in the crew.

"This was with the TMR, right?"

I pushed the wrong button. He gets this faraway look on his face, like a polar wind blowing through him. Some of it even frostbites me.

"Never. I'm talking pre-TMR. This is way before that. This is nothing with TMR. Zero."

I back off quick. "Okay. We never talked TMR. Okay?" But he's got that haunted look on his face again. He's gone very far away. I try to pull him back.

"Shane...what's the static? Where are you?"

He looks up and his eyes cut into me. It feels like he's taking me to this dark, cold place.

And then he speaks, really quietly, like he can barely get the words out.

"You know what a shadow is?"

"As in where the sun's blocked, the light can't get through?"

He gazes at me, his eyes like black rocks, his face sad, sorrow-filled, like he's been crying for a thousand years.

He just nods. "Yeah...no light."

Suddenly I feel cold, freezing cold. Shivering, I watch him walk slowly away. I don't go after him. I know he needs to be alone. He's always alone.

Maybe this is the place I wanted him to show me. Now that I felt it, I don't know why I ever wanted to go.

Grandma looks at me. "Tommy. You don't look good. You look sick."

"I feel okay, Grandma."

"Have a doughnut. Fresh fresh."

I take it and bite. Tastes like dirt in my mouth. I start to gag.

She pounds me on the back.

"You're sick, I can tell you're sick!"

"No, I just swallowed wrong, that's all."

The phone rings, the sound splitting through my head.

She picks up.

"Hello?" Glances at me. I know who it is. "No, the check hasn't come yet. There is no check." Grandma puts her hand over the mouthpiece. "Your mother wants to speak with you."

I want to smash my hand through the phone and hit her greedy face. But I step back. "Not now, Grandma. I need some air."

Grandma nods and I go outside. I walk.

SKUD

Can't stop thinking about it. Can't stop seeing the pictures in my head, pounding through my brain. Pictures. Of her and Brad. I want to rip my eyes out, but I'm not seeing them with my eyes. I want to reach inside my skull and tear the pictures out, stick something in and jab them out. I can't stand what I'm seeing.

Since junior high, Brad's been my best friend. Would he really MG me? No. Not Brad. Not unless she gave him the open highway. If she really opened that door.

But Sheila's my pureness. My untouchable. How could she give it all away?

Another picture. She's there. Her skin. She gave it to him. I see her face. Laughing. The two of them, grabbing each other and laughing. The lights are flashing behind my eyes. I taste dirt in my mouth.

The rain starts. The sun dies, darkness begins.

I come to this street. Familiar. Focus my eyes. I see it. Her house. I robot to the door. Stare at it. How long do I stand staring? Forever. Then I reach. Watch my finger touch the bell. *Ring*. Nothing. *Ring*. Footsteps.

Behind the curtain, I'm looked at. The shadow is her.

"Hi, Sheila. Here I am."

No sound from the other side. Then I hear that voice.

"Tommy?"

"Yeah. I missed you."

"It's late. Nobody's home."

"That's okay. I just…wanna talk."

"You're all wet."

"It's raining."

"You look cold."

"I am."

"You'll get sick standing out there."

And *Click*. The door opens. Sheila standing there.

I go to kiss her. She stops me. "You said you just wanted to talk."

"That's right."

We go inside and she gives me a towel. I rub my hair and send vibrations through my head. I hear pinging bounce around against the bone.

"So school?" We talk about it and she tells me how she memorizes lines.

"I write them all out with no punctuation on a sheet of paper, and then I…"

The chitty-chat goes on for twenty-five thousand hours. She's talking but I'm not hearing the words. I'm just seeing her mouth move, and her tongue skimming over her teeth, moistening her lips. The light seems to go dimmer. Little rays of light flare out of the lamp directly into my pupils and then words puke out of me like a uranium-tipped projectile.

"Did you and Brad…?"

She turns red. "You and I had something. It didn't work so it ended. Then you skulk around me like you're stoned. And now you show up, drowning in rain, to ask that?"

SKUD

"Yes. Did you do Brad?"

Now she's even redder. "None of your business." Flaring up angry. "I think you'd better go."

Business. None of mine. I feel my insides turning steam. Turning, burning. "What did you do to him?"

"Nothing. Her voice is flat, her eyes are flat.

"How did he touch you?"

"He didn't."

"How did you touch him."

Her face is drawn in. I can see her falling away from me, falling, falling.

"Get out," she says.

I take her hand. She pulls away.

"Let go."

But I don't. I can't. She's positive, I'm negative, the magnetic pull is too strong.

"Stop it!"

She let him in like she never let me, loved him like me never. She's gonna love me now.

"No!"

No, no, no, not me. Not good enough me. But I know you. I know everything. What you did.

What you did.

What you did.

What you did.

Then it's over. She's crying. Soft like the mist-rain that goes all day, every day for weeks on end. No mountains, no sea, no sun. Just dark clouds forever and drizzle dew falling down.

"Was I as good?"

She doesn't look up. She's crying, her face down. I try to kiss her but she turns her head. I see the marks I put on her arms, her neck. Bruises.

So I leave. I walk home slow, letting the sky tears fall over me, washing me. Wherever I see puddles I put my feet, let the water slip into my shoes so they fill up, my toes sliding. I sit for a long time on a curb, watching the Walk/Don't Walk sign. Nobody's walking or not walking but it keeps changing. Over and over. And a whistling sound so blind people know when it's safe to walk. I wait for the whistle and shut my eyes. I cross. Safe, like a blind man.

After half an hour, an hour, two hours, I run my tongue over my gums. I can taste doughnut. And little hard bits of stone. Doughnuts and gravel. I start to walk home. To Grandmother's house I go.

I see the red lights flashing before I even turn the corner. Two police cars in front of the building. I think run, then I think stay. I close my eyes and cross. Open them and an officer of the law is looking at me. And I look at him. His eyes register my face. His hand moves to his gun.

Certain things you look for in life. Health, happiness, prosperity.

Health is relative. You can be physically healthy but your mind can be

147

SKUD

crippled, like Tommy's. I have health. And my mind is perfect.

Happiness? This is also a relative thing. I could be happier. I'm sure most people could. But when I look around me at the sick-sore morons that lurch down these hallways, I know I'm a very, very happy man indeed. But I'll be happier when I start walking down my life's new road.

Prosperity? At the moment, I'm just starting out. But I'm working on it. In fact, the key to my new-found prosperity is just coming out of school right now. My soon to be good, good friend, Andrew.

As he passes by the Cage, I call out to him.

"Andy!"

I reach in my pocket and pull out the prize.

"Dad's watch, Andy. Healed!"

He doesn't run. Good sign. In fact, there's a little bounce in his step. He moves to me. Takes the watch. Puts it to his ear.

"Ticks," is all he says.

"Reborn," I tell him. Then I ask my leading question. "So, what's the traffic between you and Shane?"

"Usual," he replies. "And Tommy?"

I shake my head. "I don't know what got into the boy." Tombo truly is a puzzle.

"I hear Sheila's out of the hospital. They just kept her overnight for tests."

"She'll live but Soldier Boy may be gone for a while. Where's Shane?"

"Out picking flowers."

Scoob gives me a knowing look. He's grown up, this boy. It's unsettling how well he reads me.

"I don't get him," I say. "Shane had it all and walked away from it. The cars, the clothes, the girls, the rush. He was moving. Him and his brother had wings."

All of a sudden Andy's leaning in, all ears.

"You know his brother?"

I nod, wondering if he's just playing dumb with me. But there's no reason holding out on him. Shane's brother's demise is in the public domain.

"He was gunned down in some premium firefight."

The Scoober sighs. "What's the interest, Brad?"

I shrug, playing it as pulled back as I can. "I wouldn't mind being cut in."

"Into what?" he says, playing genuinely innocent.

"Into whatever you guys got going. I want some, Andy. Let me in."

Scoob gives me a curious look. "I don't get it. What happened to hockey?"

The sour taste comes back up my throat. Has he really not heard?

"Screw hockey," I scowl. "Hockey's skud."

"But you're the guy."

I say it so he'll know I'm never looking back. "Hockey's scabbed. It's pus. I want to hook up with you and Shane."

Scoob looks up in the air. Then at me.

"There's a small problem," he says. "Trust."

SKUD

Ah, trust. That stinking, pus-filled lying word. But he wants it. And to get in, I have to give. To join up, I have to prove myself.

"Test," saith I.

Andy seems interested. "Now?"

"Now."

Andy looks me up and down. He's thinking hard. I have no fear. Anything he throws at me I know I can take. I'd walk on red-hot coals, broken glass, to make this happen. I've got no other options.

Then he speaks. "The belt," he announces.

I point at my waist. "This belt?"

"Correct."

A strapping? I look forward to it. I hope he can hit hard. I wonder if I'll feel it. I want to feel it.

I remove the belt and give it to him. He snaps it.

"Where?" I ask him.

"Make some space," he says, so I take off my jacket. "Continue," he says. I remove my shirt and start to bend over, ready for the lashes.

"Keep going," he says, snapping the belt again.

What does he want? My shoes? I look down at them. He nods. So off come the shoes.

"More," says Andy.

I look at him. "Are you maxxing me?"

"So it appears," he states, just as a small group drifts by the fence and watches with eyes curious.

I take off my pants. Just gonch remain. Andy brings the stinking, muck-filled garbage can over to me.

"No deposit, no return," he says.

I take off my gonch, revealing my match in all its glory. And drop all my clothes into the can.

"What now?" I ask.

"That's everything," he says.

"So what's the plan?" I ask.

He flicks the belt. I almost welcome it to warm me up. Then he tosses it in the can.

"We'll be in touch," he says, and leaves.

All eyes are on me.

"What? What!" I snarl at the nosy crowd. They rush away. I lift out my stinking apparel, wondering what happens next. It better be good.

TOMMY They took my belt away. No socks, no clothes that I can use to hang myself. Not even a coin I can sharpen on the wall to slit my wrists.

My grandma keeps trying to visit me but I won't see her. I don't want to look at her crying face. I don't want to have to hear her ask why this happened. I don't want her to say: how could you.

How do I explain it was the Serpent? It burst through the armor, cracked the shell and I did something bad.

I love Sheila. I would never hurt her. Why did I hurt her?

SKUD

They keep asking me how a role model like me could do such a thing. I told them. I spilled all. How she was mine, how she wasn't mine. How I turned invisible. How Brad tore off her wings. How I turned into a robot. How much I love her still. And now she hates me forever.

I said to them. Kill me now.

But they just look at each other with this bored look, like they've heard that a million times before.

One eye on the wall. The camera. Never sleeps, never blinks. Just watches me 24-7 until they decide what to do with me.

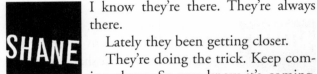

I know they're there. They're always there.

Lately they been getting closer.

They're doing the trick. Keep coming closer. So you know it's coming, you just don't know when. Makes it hard to sleep, keeps you moving. If you stay in one place too long they'll find you.

They do it to wear you down. To put the fear in you. To make you so afraid your pants are brown by the time the delivery comes. But no fear goes in me. I lost that with my brother.

Then they come. But they didn't expect the welcoming. I was more ready than they were.

They come skulking at my crash place, the tool

shed at Andy's park. Kick open the door. But I'm not there. I'm on roof. I jump down, take out two, but there are two left. I hurt them, they run, then one turns and points his gun. Fires.

I almost feel warm going to Andy's. His house is dark, but I know where his room is. I open his window. Warm air floats out on me. I crawl in. The room smells clean, like laundry soap. Andy sleeps so soft, barely breathing. He has the same hair. I stroke it, hardly touching it with my palm. He moves a little so I shake him. His eyes open. Same eyes.

"What are you doing here?"

"Talk."

"What time is it?"

"Late."

He starts to come out of the sleep a little. He looks at me.

"You look like crap."

He sits up. Feels my hand. "You're cold. Here's a blanket."

He gets up and wraps me in the blanket. It feels good.

"You're tucking me in?"

Andy laughs.

It's the same laugh, and tonight I decide to tell him.

"You laugh like him."

Andy stares at me. Like he's starting to understand.

"Same. And eyes."

SKUD

"Your brother?"

I nod.

"He always said the clock was ticking. That the Hurt we put out would come back on us. Like Karma."

"What did he mean?"

"He was stoned, reading it in a comic. I was ripped, couldn't stop laughing when he said it. Nothing was gonna catch up with us. We were so high no one could take us down. Sometimes we made six hundred bucks a day. Once we scored a thousand. We didn't ask questions. If they said torch this building or trash this car or kick this guy's head in, we did it. Better than anybody. We were mutants, man. We had the power. It was like the sea parted when we walked in a room. If we wanted something, we just took it. You know what that feels like? To be Superman?"

Andy shakes his head. He has no idea. I like that he has the guts to admit it.

"Then it happened. Don't know how. Some guy, a wannabe. What'd he want? I wannabe you. I wannabe in. I get in if I take you out. Something like that. It was a dance, a bunch of us hanging out front, smoking, snorting whatever. Feeling great. We were joking about smashing my stepdad's teeth in, then giving him the money for the dentist. The wannabe comes up to us, grinning. Pulls out this long bread knife. One of those flimsy things from a dollar store with a plastic handle. My brother's making big eyes at him, going, oooh we're scared, man, and pretending to shake. He got me laughing so hard I dropped my beer. Everybody's laughing and the kid was laughing too, but nervous like... And then he slides the knife into my brother's gut.

"My brother hardly felt it. Like a sting. Pulls it out and starts chasing the little punk with it. Never saw him run so fast. He was pissed. Who was this nobody? Finally he corners the kid. Grabs his ear. Nice earring, he says. And cuts it off. The kid screams, didn't know how lucky he was. Then my brother falls, passes right out."

Andy is shocked. "Jesus. I heard he got shot in some big fire-fight."

I want him to see what I've seen. So he'll know that's not how it happens. The truth is way smaller. Way stupider. Most people die for walking the wrong way, looking the wrong way, laughing the wrong way.

"I went in the ambulance with him. He wasn't talking. Just staring out in space. Don't know if he could hear me. The doctors kept me downstairs at the hospital. Wouldn't let me know what was going on. Till finally I just said screw this and snuck into a closet, put on an orderly's jacket. Took the elevator up to the operating room. I wanted to know what was happening, but it couldn't be bad. It was puny bread knife, a buck and a half at the store. My brother hardly felt it. What could it do?

"I came out the elevator into a hallway. Through

155

SKUD

the glass I could see all the nurses and doctors huddled around this guy on the operating table. He was cut open from his neck to his crotch. The skin and ribs spread right apart. You could see all his insides. Heart, lungs, intestines. All of it.

"And them with the tubes and sponges and needles, trying to stitch up wherever that knife had sliced. He looked something like my brother but it wasn't him. It was this guy with gray skin. Gray like a raining sky. Only it wasn't raining water. The floor was all red. All their feet were red from walking in it. Like a flood had happened in that room, an overflow, filling up with my brother's blood.

"At the funeral, he looked really nice. Sewed him all together, put him in a suit, lots of makeup. Hair combed nice. This lady came up to me, said he looked serene. He did look kinda peaceful. But all I could see was that gray face staring, chest split open, and that ocean of red that came out of him for a buck forty-nine."

 I can't find words. A million things fly through my head, a million things I want to say, but everything seems so stupid. The only words that counted were the ones Shane used telling me his story. They were the most words I ever heard him use. Maybe the most words he ever used his whole life. I finally understand what happened to his brother and why he always had that haunted look and why Shane picked me. It makes me feel scared and special and sad all at the same time.

I want to say a million things to him. But only two words come out. "I'm sorry."

He's looking so pale he's almost white, like a ghost.

And he just says, "Nothing to do with you. He took it. Now it's my turn."

"No, come on, you worry too much."

Shane's eyes are steady on me. "The Hurt you put out stays alive. Floats in the air for weeks, months, years. And one day, any day, finds you again. Doesn't care if you're bad or good now. Just smells you and splatters your life away. That's how it works."

I look at his hand. It's shaking. He's shivering.

"You're cold." I go to fix the blanket and I see it. Blood. Soaked right through the blanket. Through his clothes. Dripping on the floor.

"Shane, what is this?"

"The Hurt found me."

"It looks bad."

He shrugs.

"Don't move, I'm getting you help. Hang on, okay? Hang on."

He smiles at me. "You worry too much."

Ambulance comes quick. They strap him in and take him away. I ask the medic if he's gonna be okay.

"Hard to say with this wound, but he's young. He should pull out of it."

SKUD

My mom doesn't go whack over the scene. In fact, she just gets calmer. That's how she is, really good in crisis. It's normal life she can't handle. She only asks me three questions.

"Is this the guy who was protecting you?"

"Yes."

"Do you know what happened?"

"Not really."

"Were you involved?"

"No. I don't think he had anywhere else to go."

She nods and tells me to get dressed, she'll take me to the hospital. She drops me off as they're wheeling him in.

It's all rush rush rush. I keep going up to the desk asking how he's doing but nobody'll talk to me. It's driving me nuts until I realize I know exactly what to do.

I flip into the hallway and find a closet where a bunch of orderly jackets are hanging. Then I find my stairwell and go up the four floors. I come out into the hallway and move toward the windows.

Through the glass I can see him, plugged into a million tubes. A bunch of doctors and nurses crowded around the table. But they're not doing anything. They're just looking grim and talking. They all stare at this one guy, the surgeon, I guess. After a minute, he nods and they start unplugging Shane. Then one of the doctors puts a sheet over Shane's face and they all walk away.

A nurse steps out of the room and I run up to her. She gives me a puzzled look.

"Do you work here?"

"Yeah," I say, "all the time."

She sighs. I can tell she knows the truth.

"Was he a friend of yours?"

"Yeah," I nod. "What happened? He was doing fine when they picked him up."

"He lost a lot of blood," she says, "but it is a puzzle."

"Why?"

"I've seen people in much worse shape pull out of it. They just have to fight. But your friend, he wouldn't. There was no fight in him at all."

 So sad about Tommy. He hid his demons for so long and then he just snapped. I regret that he overreacted to my little tease, but I don't blame myself. Though I do worry about him and his precarious future. A true fall from grace.

They didn't keep him in the real jail for very long. Now he's in the Youth Detention Center, a comely building with rolling fields of grass around it and a handsome high electric fence. This is where I go to see him. I wait in the visitors' room, a bright, warm place. A guard brings him in and he sits across from me, looking a little pale.

"I see they let you dress in normal clothes here," I notice. "Maybe the place isn't too bad."

"Food's okay."

SKUD

"Lot of watching your back?"

"All you do is watch your back. Except in group therapy."

"So they counsel you? They're improving you?"

Tombo shifts in his seat, looking uncomfortable.

"Self-awareness," he says. "Anger management. And other things."

"Why would you want that?" I ask.

He glares at me. "Why do you think?"

I ignore the obvious hostility. "How long are you in for?"

"I have another psychiatric evaluation. Depending how it goes, I'll have two years in here. Then two years' probation. As long as I continue treatment."

"Reality is too harsh," I sympathize. "What did the Commander say?"

Tombo's face clouds over. "What do you expect? I'm finished."

"Ouch." This is true sadness for my compadre. All the boy ever wanted was his wings. "What now?" I ask.

He looks down at his feet. "I can try to enlist on release. But they'll never let me fly."

"That's not all bad news. There's still the premium weaponry."

He shakes his head. "Infantry is on the ground."

I try to perk my amigo up. This could be much, much worse. If he was a year older, he could be doing ten years' hard time.

"But infantry's still got cannons, tanks, grenade

launchers," I tell him. "In fact, after graduation, I'm thinking of enlisting."

"You?"

"Yeah," I say. "This thing I was hoping would happen died, so I'm on the look-out for something else. Military could fit the bill. They keep talking about invading more countries. It might be fun. We could do some war together."

I thought this news might perk him up, us enlisting together, but he only shakes his sorry head. "I just wanted to fly."

It's a tough life. Here he is, wings clipped forever, because of one fatal mistake, one misplaced deed. I see his sad face, the storm cloud raining on his head, and decide it's time to clear the air.

"Guess you're pretty pissed with me."

"Not anymore," he says.

"You know I never touched her," I say unto him.

Tommy looks up at me, his eyes piercing me.

"Yes, you did," he says, completely dead serious.

"No," I tell him. "I was pulling your chain. I never thought you'd believe me."

"You did. You did."

I'm being buzzed by his stare and beginning to think he really has hit the exit. Tommy truly has gone whack.

"Are you deaf, Tombo? I told you my hands are clean."

"No," he says, and his eyes won't break their hold

161

on me. "You put skrunk on her. You took away her name."

"What is this skud pouring from your mouth?"

"Her name's Sheila. Sheila." replies he. "This is what I have to remember."

I laugh, trying to leaven the situation. "Whatever. I'll come see you next week."

"Don't bother. I don't want to see you again." And he stands up and goes. Interview over.

Here I am, trying to set the record straight, relieve him from all pain, and his finger points at me. Like I don't know her name? Like I put skrunk on her? He requires many more hours of group therapy. Two years in here will do him good. By the time he comes out, he'll want me for a friend again. And by then I'll be his drill captain.

ANDY Whenever I shut my eyes, I feel a hand smoothing my hair. I open them and see Shane's gray face. He keeps flashing behind my eyes.

I hardly knew him. I mean, if you think about it, he was truly a rats-on-your-spine kind of guy. But he was my friend. Maybe the first real friend I ever had. I reminded him of his brother.

It's like this big sadness sitting inside me. I can't shake it. I see him when I'm sleeping, I see him when I'm awake.

I walk the sidewalks going past places where we hung. Go in, look, just to see. I walk to the park he found me in, half expecting to see him appear the way he always did. But the swings are empty, there's nobody on the monkey bars, just rain drizzling and metal against the bare trees. I keep going.

I never had a feeling like this, one I couldn't kick. Always seemed nothing mattered, nothing was for real. But he was real, and now he's not. I keep walking, trying to lose this lump in my gut but it's growing, this heavy thing inside me. Once in a while I think I hear his voice, and I turn but there's no one there. I want so bad for him to be standing there. Looking at me with those faraway eyes.

Then I look up and see where I am. Sheila's house. She hasn't been back to school since the Tommy thing happened. I stand outside wondering why I'm here.

Then I see her in the window. She motions for me to come in.

She looks the same, maybe a little pale. Her eyes are even more beautiful and sad than usual.

"I heard about Shane," she says.

Weird, but knowing what she's been through makes it easier to talk about it.

"Shane knew it was coming. Whenever I was with him, I could tell he was watching and waiting. But I had no idea."

I tell her more, about how he saved my skin, took me under his wing. How he came to me that night.

SKUD

His face. His story. The blood. And him dead on the table.

"No wonder you're going crazy," she says. "All that'd mess anybody up."

"That's not it. I miss him. He was my friend."

She nods. I look at her and realize what a piece of skud I am.

"I'm pouring it all out," I say, "but everything happened to you. You got hurt. Bad. I'm really sorry."

"Why?" she asks. "You didn't rape me. The guy who did went to jail."

She pops open a can of Pepsi. "I never should have let him in. I felt sorry for him."

I wonder if she'll ever get over what Tommy did to her.

She throws her head back, swills down the rest of her pop, then crushes the empty can in her hand. And looks at me.

"I'll get over it. But I'll never forget. I'll never be the same." Then she stares at me with those X-ray eyes. "You'll never be the same either, will you?"

I can only nod. I'm not sure, but I think she might be right.

"Why do these things happen?" I ask. "Why is everything so screwed up?"

Sheila is quiet for a while. Then she says, "I heard when Beirut was at its worst, some walls were so shot with bullet holes, you could push your hand through solid brick. It just crumbled into powder."

I look at her, not quite sure what this is about.

"A reporter asked some gunners why they kept shooting even though the enemy was gone. 'Why not?' they said. 'We still have plenty of bullets.'"

"I don't get it," I say.

"That's why I like you," she replies and throws the crushed can across the room and it swooshes into the garbage bin.

A while later I leave and realize what day it is. Wednesday. I look at my watch. I have to be somewhere. The audition with the Brothers Qualm.

I stumble through Gastown, pinballing through a busload of tourists who are craning at the steam clock. I crane too and then steam pours out as it makes this high-pitched whistle. The tourists all smile and click their disposable cameras.

I go up the elevator and everything's in slow motion. I don't want to be here. The whole thing is bogus, stupid, rank. And here I am, faking it in front of a bunch of phony Hollywood wanks so we can all cash in doing the same kind of skud that inspired the wannabe who wasted Shane. It's like spitting on Shane's grave.

The doors open and there are no big crowds of pretend bangers. Just a couple of people standing around talking.

The casting assistant spots me.

"Andy!" she yells and rushes over. "I have some new sides for you to read."

She hands me the paper, and I sit down and look at it.

SKUD

INT. ROCCO'S PLACE – NIGHT

A young-looking PUNK, all pills and attitude, shuffles in. Rocco nonchalantly looks up.

> ROCCO
> What do you got for me?

> PUNK
> Here.

He hands Rocco some money.

> ROCCO
> Is that everything?

The Punk hesitates, then pulls another fistful of cash out of his pocket.

> PUNK
> Here.

> ROCCO
> You're still short.

The Punk lifts an eyebrow.

> PUNK
> Yeah?

ROCCO
You're way short.

In a flash, the Punk pulls a KNIFE out.

ROCCO
Still short.

Rocco grabs his jacket off the chair and wraps it around his fist, using it to ward off the thrusting knife. The Punk kicks Rocco, then swipes at him, grazing his shoulder. Rocco uses his protected hand to bat the knife out of the Punk's hand. The Punk dives for it. Rocco busts a chair over the Punk's head. The Punk is still.

ROCCO
Damn. I liked that chair.

So this is the rewrite. They exchanged bullets for a phony knife fight. I start to go back to the elevator. But just as I head over, these two guys come out of the washroom. The Brothers Qualm. Only they've changed their look. The chin beards and denim are gone. Now their hair's spiked and they each sport a bullring in their twin noses.

"Andy, right? I'm Dean," he says.

The other one, Morgan, looks at me. "So what'd you think of the rewrite?"

I hesitate. Then I decide, why not?

SKUD

"It sucks," I say. "It's wank."

Their necks snap back like I slapped them. They look at each other stunned. Then Morgan turns to me.

"What didn't work for you?"

"The whole thing, man. It's stupid. It's pulp, it's all wrong."

They both breathe. Morgan Qualm looks at Dean Qualm.

"He's right," he says to his brother. "I can't believe we were so stupid."

Dean nods. "We got lost, we got waylaid."

Morgan shakes his head. "The knife was a mistake. I knew it!"

"Mea culpa," admits Dean and looks at me. "What did you think of the knife, Andy?"

I remember what Shane told me.

"You're never ready for a knife," I tell them and start to go.

"Wait! Wait!" yells Morgan. "I understand what you're saying. Knives, guns – this is not the kind of movie we want to make. Don't get us wrong, Andy. We're aiming way, way higher than that."

I nod. "Good."

Morgan's passionate. "I mean, what kind of messages are we putting out there?"

"Exactly," says Dean. "What are we saying to people?"

"We have a social responsibility," adds Morgan.

Dean holds his head. "How could we be so immoral?"

Morgan sighs. "We betrayed everything we believe in."

Then, out of the darkness, a light goes on in Dean's eyes. He turns to his twin. "We should have gone with the meat hook."

Morgan thinks for a second. He starts to grin. "Definitely. The meat hook."

They hug each other. "The meat hook!"

Morgan puts his arm around me. "Thanks, Andy, you got us back on track. Did you see your other scenes?"

"Not yet," I say.

"Don't worry about it," he says. "Now that you tote a hook, we'll have to tweak all your scenes. Then you can tell us where we live."

They take me into another room to get measured by the costume person. As she wraps me in measuring tape, I'm standing there, stunned.

I was walking from this, I swear I was walking. But instead I'm getting my costume made.

The phone rings and it's handed to me. Preston.

"Andy! My man! Congratulations!"

"Thanks," I mumble.

"You are in with the Brothers Qualm, dude! You're not just in, they love you! I love you! You are loved!"

He hangs up and I finish with the measuring thing and head home. I'm supposed to be walking on air but I'm slagging through sludge. Is this some kind of bad joke? Everything Shane taught me,

169

everything that happened to him is what got me the part. It's everything I wanted, my dream come true. Only problem is, I don't know what my dream is anymore.

I walk to the corner of Hastings and Main. I step over a drunk, and a junkie asks me for some coin, which I give him. I sit down at the bus shelter next to an old lady and her shopping bags. She's been buying groceries in Chinatown. I can see she's been crying.

"Are you all right?" I ask her.

"My grandson," she says. "He got himself into trouble."

"That's too bad," I say. "Will he be all right?"

She puts her handkerchief to her mouth. "Maybe they'll help him, I don't know. But he had so much to look forward to. Now I don't know what will happen."

I shake my head. "I had a dream once. Then it came true. And it's no good."

"Maybe you just had the wrong dream."

I look at the deep wrinkles around her face and nod. "Guess so. But now I don't have a dream anymore."

She smiles and pats me on the leg. "Don't worry, son. You'll find another one." She reaches into her big pocket and pulls out a paper bag. "Have a doughnut," she says. "Homemade."

It smells good, covered in icing sugar and cinnamon.

I take a big bite. I didn't realize how hungry I was. It's delicious.

SKUD

ACKNOWLEDGMENTS

This novel was inspired by my 1994 play, *War*, whose characters kept haunting me. I wanted to give them a larger canvas, to dig deeper into their actions, to spend more time with them. In many ways, that play was the first draft of this book.

I would like to thank Elizabeth Dancoes for her impeccable advice and encouragement. Thanks also to Guillermo Verdecchia, Shelley Tanaka, Green Thumb Theatre, and the many teenagers, social workers, police officers, psychologists and teachers who shared their time. I am indebted to the Rosalind Miles book, *The Rites of Man*, which continues to resonate. As she states, "manhood training by its very nature creates the climate in which violence can flourish, and a society in which, despite its pious protestations, a level of violence is always tolerated, indeed expected. Boys will be boys."